The Greek Symbol Mystery

"Where's George?" Bess gasped.

"I don't know," Nancy whispered, completely mystified.

Several hundred yards away, an engine purred, then roared off quickly. Leaving their post in front of Vatis's cottage, Nancy and Bess raced up the road toward their taxi and leaped in.

"Follow that car, please," Nancy implored the driver, and pointed to the pair of taillights that were fast disappearing down the hill.

"Our friend has been kidnapped!"

Nancy Drew Mystery Stories

Available from Wanderer Books

NANCY DREW MYSTERY STORIES ®

THE GREEK SYMBOL MYSTERY

by
Carolyn Keene

WANDERER BOOKS

Published by Simon & Schuster, New York

Copyright © 1981 by Simon & Schuster, Inc.
All rights reserved
including the right of reproduction
in whole or in part in any form
Published by WANDERER BOOKS
A Division of
Simon & Schuster, Inc.
Simon & Schuster Building
1230 Avenue of the Americas
New York, New York 10020

Manufactured in the United States of America
10 9 8 7 6 5

NANCY DREW and NANCY DREW MYSTERY STORIES,
WANDERER and colophon are registered trademarks of
Simon & Schuster, Inc.

Library of Congress Cataloging in Publication Data
Keene, Carolyn, pseud.
The Greek symbol mystery.
(Her Nancy Drew mystery stories; 60)
SUMMARY: Her friends Bess and George accompany
Nancy to Greece where there are two mysteries they want
to solve.
[1. Mystery and detective stories. 2. Greece—
Fiction] I. Sanderson, Ruth. II. Title.
PZ7.K23Nan   no. 60   [Fic]   80-39778
ISBN 0-671-42297-9
ISBN 0-671-63891-2 (pbk.)

Contents

1

Mystery Plus Mystery

"Nancy, do you think you could help solve a mystery for me while you're in Greece?" asked Mrs. Thompson, a friend and neighbor of the Drews. A tinge of sadness crept into the woman's hazel eyes.

"Oh, I'd love to," the titian-haired eighteen-year-old replied. "What's it about?"

Nancy's father, Carson Drew, a well-known River Heights attorney, had just given her an intriguing assignment to follow up in Athens. Now the young detective would have two mysteries to solve!

"I'll explain," said Jeannette Thompson, seeing the excitement in Nancy's face. "I've been sending money to the Papadapoulos family for about a year, but the last few payments disappeared."

1

"Disappeared?" Nancy repeated. "Were they stolen?"

"I don't know. I didn't send the money directly to Greece. There was an agency in New York—the Photini Agency—which transferred my donations. The main office is in Athens, and I assume that Mr. Georgiou, the New York manager, forwarded the money to Athens. Then it went to the family."

"You say that some of the money disappeared," Nancy went on. "Do you mean the family never received it?"

"That's right," Mrs. Thompson replied. "I used to get very sweet thank-you notes from the mother, but they stopped coming. Then, last week, I heard from her again. Mrs. Papadapoulos said she was writing because she had not heard from me in so long! Apparently, she contacted the Photini Agency in Athens about the missing payments. They told her that probably I had lost interest. Can you imagine such a thing?"

Nancy shook her head in bewilderment. "No, I can't," she said. "What about the New York office?"

"It closed suddenly."

Mrs. Thompson explained that she had tried to telephone Mr. Georgiou several times but there was never any answer. "I finally asked the police to investigate, and that's how I found out the office had closed. According to the post office, all mail was to be sent to Mr. Georgiou in care of the Athens address."

"What's his first name?" Nancy asked.

"Dimitri."

"Did he endorse your checks?"

"Yes, with the name of the Photini Agency stamped underneath," the woman said. "I can show you one."

Mrs. Thompson disappeared into her bedroom and soon returned with a small metal box. It contained numerous cancelled checks. She leafed through them quickly.

"Here you are," she said, handing one to the young detective.

Nancy stared at the signature on the back. It was bold and distinctive. Obviously it belonged to a person of confidence.

"Did you ever meet Mr. Georgiou?" Nancy asked.

"No. All the arrangements were made through the mail. I had seen an ad to sponsor needy children in Greece and that's how it all started. There are three children in the Papadapoulos family, but my donations were primarily intended to help send Maria to school."

Nancy's mind was racing. Had Dimitri Georgiou kept the money for himself? How many other poor

3

Greek families had he robbed? Or had someone else taken the money? But who?

Nancy squeezed Mrs. Thompson's hand. "We'll do all we can," the girl detective assured her.

"We?" the woman asked.

"My friends Bess and George are going with me," Nancy explained.

Bess Marvin and George Fayne were cousins and Nancy's closest friends. They often helped her solve mysteries, even those in distant countries.

"Well, my dear, is there anything else I ought to tell you?" Mrs. Thompson asked.

"I'd like to make a copy of Dimitri Georgiou's signature," Nancy said. She pulled a small notepad and a felt-tip pen from her handbag, then carefully imitated the handwriting. "Clue number one," she said, slipping the pad and pen back into her bag.

When Nancy reached home that afternoon, she immediately called Bess and George to report her visit with Mrs. Thompson. "So," she concluded, "between looking for Helen Nicholas's cousin, her missing inheritance, and Mrs. Thompson's money, we'll have plenty to do in Athens!"

"I'll say," George replied. "I can't wait!"

Hannah Gruen, the Drews' housekeeper who had helped rear Nancy since she was three years old, when her mother had passed away, overheard the conversation. "Your trip sounds like trouble to me," she said, frowning.

4

"Oh, Hannah," Nancy said, chucking the woman's chin affectionately. "You worry so."

When the young detective and her friends boarded the plane for New York the next day, she grinned. "Last night Hannah dreamed that we'd be greeted at Athens airport by gorgons—monsters with snakes for hair!"

Plump Bess Marvin ran a hand through her blond waves and shivered. "Thanks for telling me. I'm nervous about flying as it is."

George laughed. "Didn't you say Hannah was having a permanent today, Nancy? I bet that's what inspired the nightmare!"

As the three girls settled into their seats, George yawned. "How long do we have to wait in New York between flights?" she asked Nancy.

"Three hours."

"In that time," Bess said, "we could take a sightseeing tour of the whole city."

"That's just what I had in mind," Nancy said.

The cousins looked at her in surprise. "Are you serious?" George asked.

Nancy nodded. "Here's the address of the Photini Agency in Astoria. We might pick up a clue."

"Out there? We'll miss our plane!" Bess objected.

"No, we won't."

"Didn't you know that every New York taxi has wings?" George chuckled.

"Just so long as ours has four good tires," Bess replied.

The flight to New York took little more than an hour. Within twenty minutes after landing, the trio had flagged down a cab. It looped onto a service road that fed into a busy highway.

"That's the building over there," the taxi driver said, taking the exit for Astoria.

Bess gaped at a line of people holding signs and marching up and down the block.

"Who's on strike?" George asked.

"The tenants," their driver replied as they pulled close.

Nancy took some money from her wallet and handed it to the man. "We'll get out here. Thanks."

"Not me," Bess said. "I'm going back to the airport."

As George nudged her cousin out the door, Nancy caught sight of the storefront that bore the name PHOTINI. A peppery-haired man was sweeping out the empty store.

"Let's talk to him," Nancy suggested.

But as they started to slip through the picket line, brusque voices shouted at them. "Hey, where do you think you're going?" one cried out. "Yeah, that's what I want to know!" yelled the other.

George stared into a pair of angry eyes. "We're only trying to—" she began apologetically.

The man behind them snapped like a firecracker. "Say, who are you anyway?" he asked George. "You look like Mr. Sully's daughter!"

"That's her, all right," another man added in an accusing tone. "You tell your father we're going to see that all his buildings are condemned by the city!"

"She's not—" Nancy interrupted, but was cut off as the crowd pressed closer to the girls. She grabbed George by one arm while Bess hung onto the other.

"We're cousins," she murmured. "Her name is Fayne and mine is—"

Her words trailed off as the men barked back. "Go home, Miss Sully. We're the new landlords here!"

The men laughed harshly, forcing the girls to step off the curb into the street.

"Those men aren't going to let us within two feet of that agency," George declared.

"I knew we should've stayed at the airport," Bess put in as the cleaning man retreated into the store.

"Let's go," Nancy said in disappointment. She waved to an oncoming taxi. "I hope our batting average improves when we get to Athens."

The girls were still discussing the side trip when they boarded their plane, an Olympic Airways jet. While Bess went ahead to find their seats, Nancy stopped to talk with the copilot. He was young and had dark hair that spun in waves across his forehead.

"I flew a small plane once," Nancy told him. "I can't imagine sitting behind controls like these."

"Well, as long as we aren't in motion yet," the copilot replied, ducking into the front compartment, "be my guest."

"Oh, are you sure it's all right?"

"Just don't touch anything. Okay?"

She nodded and slipped into the comfortable bucket seat next to him. "This is fantastic!" Nancy exclaimed, leaning toward the bank of knobs and gauges.

Suddenly a man's voice bellowed at the pair from behind them. "What is this? Some joke? You let a girl try to fly this plane? Are you crazy?"

The copilot tried to explain but could not get a word in as the angry passenger kept complaining. Finally, Nancy stood up and stared calmly at the burly man. His face was the shade of a pale tomato.

"If you're going to fly this plane," he yelled, "I'll see to it we never leave the ground!"

"You have nothing to worry about," Nancy replied. "I'm only a passenger like yourself."

"Then what are you doing in the pilot's seat?" the man demanded.

Nancy explained. She had just finished when

one of the flight attendants approached the group. "Please be seated, Mr. Isakos," she said to the man and handed him a Greek newspaper.

Instead of thanking her, he merely shrugged. "Girls should be kept in their place—certainly nowhere near the controls of an airplane!"

George, who had heard part of the conversation, was angry at the man's presumptuous tone. "In case you didn't know," she said as he walked down the aisle, "Amelia Earhart was an ace pilot and so is Nancy Drew!"

Isakos did not answer her. He slid into a seat not far from the girls.

Nancy frowned. "We'll probably have to listen to his complaints all the way to Athens!"

She purposely averted her eyes from his as she moved toward her seat. Halfway there she noticed a piece of paper on the floor. She glimpsed the name PHOTINI printed boldly in the upper left-hand corner, and picked it up.

"What's that?" Bess asked as Nancy slid into her seat next to George and fastened her seat belt.

"I don't know," Nancy said.

The three young detectives stared curiously at her discovery. It was the torn letterhead of the Greek agency that was under suspicion! Beneath the printed address was a most mysterious-looking doodle: ℘

2

Stolen Note

Instantly Nancy pulled a small magnifying glass from her handbag and trained it over the unusual doodle. "It looks like the Greek letter phi," she said.

"But what are those curlicues at each end?" Bess whispered.

"Maybe that means the doodler is going in circles!" George replied, grinning.

"Or it could mean something important," Nancy said. She strained her neck to look out the window as the plane taxied into the lineup ready for takeoff. The runway shimmered in the heat.

"Do you think it'll be this hot in Greece?" Bess asked.

"Hotter," George teased. "I've heard it gets to at least 120 degrees in the shade—"

"Of an olive tree," Nancy added absently.

Paying small attention to the light banter between her friends, she stared at the note again. Suddenly, she realized there was some faded, almost invisible handwriting on the Photini letterhead.

"Look at this!" she exclaimed, handing the piece of paper and her magnifying glass to George.

"Let me see it, too," Bess said.

"In a minute," her cousin replied. She held the glass over the words Nancy had indicated. "All I can make out is *Záppeion* and *Maïou*."

"*Záppeion*," Nancy repeated. "Isn't that the place in Athens that has a huge military exhibit?"

Her listeners shrugged. "I don't know about that," George said, "but I think *Maïou* means the month of May in Greek."

Bess was able to detect one or two more words in the message, and together they reconstructed the sentence: *rendezvous stó Záppeion tís íkosi pénde Maïou*. Nancy filled in the letters with her pen as the plane's engines began to roar and the flight attendants returned to their stations for takeoff. Once the plane was in the air, Nancy summoned one of them.

"Will you please translate this for me?" she asked, indicating the message in Greek.

The young woman wrinkled her forehead for a second, then answered. "It says 'meeting at Záppeion on the 25th of May.' That was a month ago."

"Where exactly is Záppeion?" Nancy inquired.

"It's not far from my apartment—behind the King's Garden in the heart of Athens. If you haven't been there, you ought to go."

"I'm sure we will," Bess said. "What other sight-seeing do you recommend?"

"Oh, there is so much—the National Archeological Museum or the Benaki, for instance. And you must see Plaka, the old section of Athens. Also, monastiraki, the flea market."

"Isn't that the place Helen Nicholas told us about?" Bess whispered to Nancy.

"Yes, she said it's within walking distance of our hotel."

When the flight attendant excused herself, Nancy pulled out the notepad with Dimitri Georgiou's signature. She compared it with the message on the letterhead. The formation of the letters was the same!

"So I guess we can conclude Dimitri wrote this," George said, "and met someone at Záppeion on May 25th. But who and why, and was the meeting relevant to our case?"

"The point is," Nancy said, drawing two sets of crisscrossed lines on the back of the letterhead, "whoever he wrote this to is probably on this plane."

"But we don't want him to know we're looking

for Mr. Georgiou, do we?" Bess declared. She formed an *X* in a corner box of the tic-tac-toe pattern she had just drawn.

"If you mean we shouldn't ask someone to claim the letterhead," Nancy went on, "I agree."

She and Bess played a few games of tic-tac-toe. Then dinner was served. There was a generous portion of moussaka on each tray, along with fresh green salad garnished with feta cheese and small black olives.

"I love eggplant," Bess said, savoring her last forkful.

After the meal, the girls slipped on headphones to listen to music and later to the sound track of the in-flight movie. To their delight, it had been filmed in Athens. Nancy paid less attention to the story than to the twisting alleyways the girls would investigate tomorrow!

When it was over, the lights in the plane remained dim. Restless passengers got up to stretch while others, including the young detectives, asked for pillows and blankets.

"Good night," George yawned presently.

" 'Night," Bess said.

Nancy wedged her handbag next to her, then closed her eyes, sinking soon into a deep sleep. It was only an hour or so later that she awoke as she felt her handbag being shoved against her. Groggi-

14

ly she glanced into the aisle. She saw no one there.

It must've been my imagination, she concluded, and drifted off again.

Sunlight flooded the plane a few hours later as it droned across southern Europe. It was three A.M. in New York but nine o'clock there.

"We just lost six hours," Bess yawned.

"Cheer up," her cousin replied. "You'll gain them all back when we go home."

"Promise?" the other girl said.

She closed her eyes again while Nancy opened her handbag.

"It's gone!" she cried suddenly.

"What's gone?" George asked.

"The paper—the letterhead!"

"Are you sure?" Bess put in.

"Look for yourself," Nancy said.

She pulled out her wallet, a checkbook, various cosmetics, an airplane ticket, and passport, leaving only a set of small luggage keys in the bottom of the bag. The Photini letterhead was, indeed, missing.

"Maybe you threw it away with your dinner napkin," George suggested.

Nancy shook her head. "Don't you remember we played tic-tac-toe on the back of it, then I put it into my purse before we ate?" She sank back into her seat. "Someone took it," she added.

15

She told about being half-awakened the night before when she felt the bag being moved. "But I guess I was so tired I just dismissed it."

"Don't feel bad," Bess consoled her. "At least we know that one out of all the passengers on board has contact with Dimitri."

"So all we have to do is interrogate 300 people!" George quipped.

Nancy wrinkled her nose. "You and Bess take coach and I'll go through first class," she replied, chuckling.

The girls dismissed the incident temporarily from their minds as they debarked and collected their suitcases. Outside, the sun blanketed the area of Glyfada in thick layers of heat.

"It's sweltering," George declared, feeling the temperature seeping through her sandals.

"We'll get used to it," Nancy said and darted toward a taxi stand. Within moments, the girls were on their way to the Hotel Skyros, a charming place located near Omonia Square.

"Gor-geous!" Bess exclaimed as a porter led them to their room.

It was large, with sliding glass doors that opened onto a terrace view of the Acropolis. On the walls were embroidered tapestries and beside each bed was a small flokati rug.

"When we get up in the morning," said Bess, "we'll think we're floating on an Athenian cloud!"

Nancy and George laughed as they opened their suitcases.

Nancy removed a folding umbrella and remarked, "This could have stayed home!"

Before she could unpack anything else, there was a knock on the door. The porter had returned with a basket of delicious-looking yellow apples.

"For you," he said, setting it on the table in front of the glass doors.

"Thank you," Nancy replied.

"Maybe Ned sent them," Bess suggested after the porter left, referring to Nancy's special date. "Is there a card?"

"I don't see any," Nancy said. "Perhaps it's a welcome gift from the hotel."

She was tempted to sample it but decided to hang up her clothes first. George, on the other hand, scooped an apple off the top. As she bit into it, she glimpsed something green and scaly inside the basket. It was slithering upward between the fruit! George dropped the apple on the floor and stepped back.

"There's a snake in here! Nancy! Bess!" she cried.

Now the venomous head emerged. George held her breath and took another step away as Nancy reached for her umbrella.

"Don't move!" she told George, then slid the tip of the umbrella under the reptile.

It swooped forward abruptly, then swung back again.

"Oh!" Bess shrieked. "Be careful!"

"Sh!" her cousin chided her.

Seconds ticked by slowly as Nancy edged closer, hoping to bait the snake onto the umbrella. This time, to her relief, it curled across the folds of the material.

"Get the wastebasket and one of the flokati rugs," Nancy said to Bess. "We'll use it as a cover."

Trembling, Bess obeyed Nancy's instructions. She placed the basket near the table, dropped the rug in a heap next to it, then darted out of range. Nancy turned slowly and steadily on her heels, never letting her eyes leave the poisonous creature, and lowered the umbrella into the basket.

"Whew!" she sighed in relief as the snake slid off.

Instantly George stuffed the rug over it while Nancy dialed the hotel desk.

"Someone will come to dispose of it," she told the girls.

"When?" Bess asked, still shivering.

"Soon, very soon."

As promised, a young hotel worker appeared within minutes. He did not say anything, but when Nancy handed him the wastebasket and lifted the rug, he gasped. He turned quickly and ran down the hall with it.

"Give him the apples too!" Bess said. "Porter! Porter!" she called after him, but it was too late. He had disappeared through a stairway exit.

"It's just as well," Nancy said, removing the apples from the basket. "Maybe there's something else hidden inside."

"Like a scorpion?" Bess squirmed.

"If anything, there are probably dollar bills," Nancy announced mysteriously. "Remember the Greek myth about the Golden Apples? They were guarded by a snake that twisted itself around the pillars of Heracles, and that's how the dollar sign came into being."

"I always thought apples were a love gift from Aphrodite," Bess said dreamily.

Ignoring the comment, Nancy glanced inside the basket. "Nothing here," she said, refilling it.

"So now what?" Bess asked, flopping down on her bed. "I'm beat."

"You're just suffering from delusions," George giggled. "Come on. Get up. We have work to do."

"Right this minute?" Bess muttered.

Nancy glanced at her watch. "We may be able to catch Mr. Vatis before he leaves his office," she said, referring to the attorney who handled Helen Nicholas's inheritance from her uncle.

The girls took a taxi to the address Mr. Drew had given Nancy for the law firm Vatis & Vatis. To their astonishment, the attorneys had moved and another name was painted on the entrance.

Inside, Nancy introduced herself to the receptionist, who smiled politely when she heard Nancy's question concerning the law office. "All I know is that the father, Vatis Senior, died some time ago. I have no idea where his son is. No one else does, either."

"Thank you anyway," Nancy said in disappointment.

Turning to leave, she and the others almost bumped into a man who was standing behind them apparently waiting to talk to the young woman. The girls apologized and left, a little embarrassed.

"I wonder where Vatis went," Bess remarked.

"Who knows?" George sighed. "The question is, where do we go from here?"

3

Unwanted Mask

"We're not far from Plaka," Nancy replied to Bess's question.

"Then what are we waiting for?" her friend asked. "I hear it's mysterious and exciting!"

Within ten minutes, the girls found themselves in the quaint district of old Athens where the capital of modern Greece had formed in the early 1800s.

"The houses are charming," Nancy observed.

The buildings rose in craggy steps like layers of stone carved out of an ancient hill. Most were trellised with vines and had window boxes and clay pots filled with colorful flowers. Jasmine and honeysuckle permeated the air.

"Smells wonderful," Bess said. She breathed

deeply as they wandered down the narrow, winding street.

They had paused in front of a small Byzantine church when a bearded clergyman wearing a black robe darted ahead to enter. Nancy gazed up at the faded red dome.

"It must be several hundred years old," she said. "Shall we go in, too?"

"Sure," George replied.

The odor of incense filled the church as the service ended, and in the entrance thin, white candles burned dimly, creating a soft glow around the icon on the stand next to them. It was a small wood panel on which a saint's picture had been painted. The bearded priest placed a beautiful silver box in front of it.

"What's he doing?" Bess whispered as he hurried out.

"He's leaving a present for the saint," Nancy explained. She stepped closer.

To her surprise, there was a nautical crest engraved on the lid of the box. Was the young man related to a shipping family? If so, might he know Constantine Nicholas?

"Come on!" the girl detective exclaimed, leading the way out.

By now, the Orthodox priest was far ahead of them. To Nancy's dismay, he disappeared quickly into the crowd of pedestrians at the foot of the hill.

"Oh, dear," Nancy said with a sigh as they lost sight of him completely.

The smell of roasted corn now drew the girls farther into monastiraki, where a variety of wares hung across open shop doors.

"Look at those embroidered blouses," Bess remarked. "Aren't they pretty?"

"I'm going to buy one," George announced.

"Me too," her cousin replied.

Nancy had her eye on two lovely linen tablecloths across the way. She bought them, then stopped in front of another store window. The sign above it said CHRYSOTEQUE.

"That must mean 'gold store,'" Nancy said as Bess and George caught up to her. "Just look at all that fabulous jewelry!"

Even more intriguing was the gold mask displayed in the middle!

"It's beautiful," George remarked.

The girls leaned forward for a closer look when suddenly it was pulled out of the window.

"I guess somebody wants to buy it," Bess said, and entered the shop followed by Nancy and George.

To their amazement, though, there were no customers inside. Behind a curtain at the rear, angry voices shouted at each other.

"Maybe we should leave," Bess murmured as a young boy appeared from behind the curtain and raced out of the store in tears.

Then a woman stepped into view and smiled. "May I help you?" she asked.

"I was interested in the mask in your window—" Nancy said.

"That's been sold," the shopkeeper replied curtly. "We have no more like it."

"In that case," Bess put in, "I'd like to buy this pin." She pointed to one in the form of a mask. "What do you think, girls?"

"Don't forget you have to lug all this stuff through customs," her cousin reminded her. She gazed at her friends' shopping bags. They were filling up rapidly.

"But this won't weigh a thing," Bess insisted and asked the shopkeeper the price.

"Not much at all, less than a thousand drachmas," the woman said.

"How many American dollars is that?" George inquired.

"Three—four."

"It's more like thirty," Nancy whispered to Bess.

"Even so," the girl said, "I'll take it. Somehow, spending drachmas is more fun than spending dimes!"

George rolled her eyes to the ceiling. "I'm going

to save my traveler's checks for something I really want," she said as they stepped outside. "Like a cruise on the Aegean."

By now, the girls were beginning to feel tired from their long walk. Nancy laid her heavy shopping bag on the sidewalk whenever she could. She had done so twice, and the second time the bag was nearly trampled on by tourists who window-shopped beside her.

"Let's get out of here," Bess suggested at last. "I can't take all of these people."

The girls walked toward Syntagma Square, where a din of children's voices circled an old man who wore a flat hat made of natural sponge. He carried others over his arm. They were all different shapes and sizes.

"*Barba Yanni! Barba Yanni!*" a small boy cried, eagerly trading a few coins for a big sponge.

"He sure won't need an umbrella," George said. "That sponge could soak up an entire cloudburst!"

"I'd like to soak up something cool," Bess said as they passed an ice-cream vendor.

"How about sitting down, too?" George asked.

The three found a sidewalk table. After they gave their order, a young man pulled up a chair.

"You American?" he asked in halting English.

"Yes, we are," George replied.

"I show you Athens," he announced.

"Oh, we couldn't—" Bess said.

"No, thank you," Nancy interrupted coolly.

"*Entaxi*," he said, heaving a sigh. "Okay, girls. So long."

Giggling, Bess leaned toward her friends. "I think we broke his heart," she said, watching him leave.

Instantly George changed the subject. "May we see your tablecloths?" she asked Nancy, who promptly opened her shopping bag.

"Hey, what's this?" she said, discovering an extra package. It was wrapped like the others from the jewelry store. She pulled it out and removed the paper.

"It's the gold face mask we saw in the window!" Bess exclaimed.

"How did it get into my shopping bag?" Nancy wondered.

George shrugged. "It sure looks like a real ancient piece," she replied, "not a reproduction."

She took the mask from her friend and turned it over, examining it closely. "How about this?" she declared, pointing to a gold-colored sticker affixed to the metal behind the chin.

"It's that doodle!" Nancy said excitedly.

"Doodle?"

"Yes, like the one someone drew on the Photini letterhead. It's the letter phi, but instead of curli-

26

cues at each end, this one has the head of a snake."

"The whole symbol is actually the body of a snake," Bess observed. "What do you suppose it means?"

"I don't know, but I'm going to find out," Nancy said, announcing her plan to return to the jewelry shop immediately.

"Right this minute?" Bess asked. "Can't we relax a bit longer? I really feel dizzy."

"Maybe you ought to go back to the hotel," George said, as her cousin rose unsteadily from her chair.

"I think you're right," Bess replied. "It must be the heat or something."

Nancy insisted that George accompany her cousin, adding that she would not be long at Chrysoteque's. To her disappointment, she found the jewelry store closed.

Siesta time, Nancy thought, snapping her fingers. Maybe the archeological museum could give her some information about the mask!

She took a taxi there and found it also was ready to close for a few hours. The guard at the door rattled at her in Greek as she pleaded in English to be let in.

It's no use, Nancy thought anxiously.

Then she showed him the gold mask. To her astonishment, he grabbed it from her and said something in Greek. Nancy shook her head in puzzlement. He took her arm and pulled her toward an office at the end of the corridor.

I hope he's taking me to see the curator, she murmured to herself. And I hope he speaks English!

When they stepped into the room, the guard flew past a secretary to an inner office. Seated behind a desk was a brown-haired man with a trace of gray in his sideburns. The guard spoke in Greek and laid the gold mask in front of him.

"I am in charge of this museum," he said to Nancy in a thick accent. "Who are you and where did you get this?"

The girl detective introduced herself, explaining, "I found it in my shopping bag."

"In your what?" the curator replied.

"In—"

"Just a minute," he interrupted and dialed a number on his telephone.

Within seconds, another man appeared breathless in the doorway. The curator told Nancy he was a detective who had been recently assigned to the museum after a series of art thefts.

"The mask was stolen from this museum, Miss Drew," the curator announced. "Did you know that?"

"No. How could I?"

The detective's glaring eyes made Nancy suddenly feel like a criminal.

"As a matter of fact," the curator went on, "this mask should now be in the United States with a traveling exhibit."

"You mean to different museums?" Nancy answered.

"Then," the detective interrupted in sparse English, "you know something."

"No, I—no, I don't. I was shopping at the flea market and—"

"And you bought this mask?" the curator asked.

The guard, who understood no English, remained stone-faced while the detective laughed. "A joke—she bought mask monastiraki! Ha!"

The three men conferred quietly for several minutes. The curator turned the mask over. He seemed to be making comments about the symbol on the back, then pointed accusingly at Nancy.

This is ridiculous, she thought. They think I'm a thief!

"When the thieves realized they could not sell the mask, they got rid of it," the curator stated. "Does that make sense to you, Miss Drew?"

"I suppose so. Maybe they figured you were close to catching them and planted the mask on me."

"Perhaps you belong to gang," the detective put

29

in haltingly. "You American girlfriend or cousin to one of the members?"

"No," Nancy said indignantly. Trying to remain calm, she added, "Even if I were, which I'm not, I'd hardly have stepped into such a flimsy trap."

"Even so, we must keep you here until we know otherwise!" the curator exclaimed.

4

The Intruder

As the curator spoke, a flush of anger rose in Nancy's cheeks. "You are going to hold me?" she repeated.

"That is correct, Miss Drew," he replied. "We cannot let you go, now that you have given us the first clue to the thieves. Tell us about this symbol."

"I can't—I don't know how it got on the mask or who put it there." Nancy asked if she might make a phone call to her hotel.

"You may use this telephone."

To the girl's relief, George answered on the first ring. When she heard Nancy's predicament, she was astounded.

"We'll—I mean I'll—come to the museum right away," George said. "Bess still isn't feeling well, so she'd better stay here. Bye—"

"Wait, George. Don't hang up," Nancy said anxiously. "Please call my father. He'll know what to do." She put down the receiver, hoping Mr. Drew, though thousands of miles away, would somehow come to her rescue.

George immediately asked the hotel operator to place a call to the attorney's office. She was told it could take a couple of hours to go through.

George hung up and said to Bess, "Nancy can't wait that long. I'm going downstairs to the kiosk, the magazine stand, on the corner. There's a public telephone inside."

"Shall I go with you?" Bess asked, lifting her head off the pillow.

"You stay put." George drew the half-closed drapes fully shut, then left.

Bess snuggled under the blanket and curled herself into a comfortable knot. Sleep overtook her quickly and it was not until something shuffled in front of her bed that she awakened. Groggily, she turned her head toward the door, glimpsing the back of a man as he shut the door quietly. Bess gasped. It was only the ring of the telephone that kept her from running after him.

"Hello," she said shakily.

"Where's George?" Nancy asked before Bess could tell her about the intruder. "It's been almost an hour since I talked to her."

Suddenly Bess's eyes shifted to the table where

the basket of apples had been. It was gone!

"Oh, Nancy!" she cried out. "Something awful happened!"

"To George?"

"No, no. Someone broke into our room—"

"What!"

"A man. He took the apples. I didn't get much of a look at him, but I'm not staying here another minute. I'm coming right to the museum."

Bess said good-bye, splashed cold water on her face, then dressed and grabbed her purse.

At the museum, Nancy sank into a chair in the curator's office. She thought anxiously about George, the strange intrusion at the hotel, and how she could free herself from the detective who glowered at her. Then, to her great relief, she heard a familiar voice in the corridor.

"George!" she cried, racing to the door.

The girl's short dark hair was tousled from running and she was out of breath.

"I'm sorry I took so long," George panted. "The hotel phones were tied up and the one at the kiosk was out of order. So I went to the American Embassy. I spoke to one of the attachés who—"

"And who are you?" the curator interrupted George.

"George Fayne. I'm Nancy's friend and—"

Just then Bess walked into the room. "Oh,

George, I'm glad you're here," she said, then quickly introduced herself to the curator.

"Nancy is working on a case. You have to let her go!" Bess added.

"Oh, really?" the officer snapped.

"I can prove that Nancy is a detective!" she declared.

"You're making it worse," George murmured, causing Bess to stop talking.

The general silence lasted only a few seconds. Then the curator's secretary summoned him out of the room. The detective joined them, leaving the guard to watch the girls.

"What's going on?" Bess asked.

Nancy and George shrugged. "Maybe the wheels of justice have started to turn," her cousin said.

The prediction proved correct. Nancy was released shortly, but not without a warning.

"You may be helpful to American police," the detective said, "but you are not to us. So stay out of our case."

Despite the stinging remark, Nancy smiled politely and said good-bye. Leaving the mask behind them, Bess and George followed her out of the museum.

"You're not going to give up working on the mystery, are you?" Bess asked.

"You heard what the man said," Nancy replied, but the mischievous gleam in her eyes told the others she had no intention of quitting.

Again Bess mentioned the intruder, which troubled her listeners.

"That guy may have been in our room before we returned," George said, "and slipped out onto the terrace when he heard us coming. I thought it was odd the drapes were half-closed but figured the maid had drawn them."

"What's even stranger," Bess added, "is that he took the basket of apples he probably sent us in the first place."

"That's only an assumption. Maybe the apples were intended for somebody else," Nancy pointed out.

"More likely," George put in, "the poisonous snake was. After all, who, other than our friends, knew were were coming to Greece?"

Their next stop, the girls agreed, would be the Photini Agency. It was located on the upper floor of a bank building in the heart of the city. Staff members darted from files to desks, creating an air of busyness in contrast to the vacant office in New York.

"This place sure isn't going out of business," Nancy commented, then asked to see the manager.

He was a short, friendly man with dark eyes. "I

am Mr. Diakos," he said, greeting them warmly.

Nancy introduced herself and the others, adding that they had recently visited the agency in New York.

"Ah, then you know about our poor pitiful village families," Mr. Diakos said. "They need constant help."

Apparently, Nancy thought, he thinks we're interested in sponsoring somebody.

"Here, look at her," the man went on, pulling open a desk drawer and producing a photograph of a small, sad-faced child. "Such a pretty girl, but you see? No smile."

"I—" Nancy tried to interrupt.

"And look at this one." Mr. Diakos showed her another picture. "He is her brother. They live in Athikia." Next he removed a manila folder from a second drawer. "All these children come from Angelo Kastro, another town on the Peloponnesos. Their families are very poor and—"

"Mr. Diakos, I'm afraid we are only interested in one specific family at the moment," Nancy cut in at last.

"Oh, yes?" the manager fluttered his eyelids.

"Papadapoulos is the name. They live in Agionori."

Without waiting to hear more, Mr. Diakos asked a secretary to check their file. No one by that name was listed. Puzzled, Nancy revealed Mrs. Thompson's story about the missing payments and Dimitri Georgiou's disappearance.

"Have you seen or heard from him recently?" George asked.

"No, I haven't, but that did not seem strange to me. I'm new to this position and it's taken me a while to adjust."

"Did this office send Mr. Georgiou lists of names for sponsorship on a regular basis?" Bess spoke up.

"Yes, but only a few were picked by Americans."

"What happened to the rest?"

"They still need support."

"Is it possible," Nancy suggested, "that Mr. Georgiou signed up sponsors without reporting them to you?"

"Of course, but why—how could he do such a thing? It's terrible to steal from the poor!" The idea stirred Mr. Diakos into a rage. "Dimitri Georgiou will pay for this!" he blazed angrily.

"But we're not sure he took the money," Bess said, trying to calm the man.

"Well, someone did!" he declared.

Before leaving, Mr. Diakos took the girls' hotel address and phone number. "If I hear anything about Dimitri's whereabouts, I will let you know."

"Another dead end," Bess said in disappointment. "Now what?"

"Let's go to the Nikos Shipping Company," Nancy suggested. "But first we should visit Dad's friend, Mr. Mousiadis. He might be able to lend us a car." She pulled the man's business card out of her pocket. "It's not far from the Hotel Skyros."

When they reached his office, they were met by an efficient young assistant who introduced them to Mr. Mousiadis. He was a tall, sturdy man with a pleasant face. He ushered the girls to comfortable chairs. Before Nancy needed to ask, he offered her the use of his car.

"That is very generous of you," she said. "Thank you, I—"

He lifted his hand as if to stop her from saying more. "You father told me why you are here and I am happy to help you. Unfortunately, I must leave for Italy tomorrow, so I won't be able to show you around. Even so, maybe my four wheels can!" He smiled broadly. "But I have a suggestion for you."

"What is it?" Bess asked.

"If you have time, please buy a *máti*, an amulet to protect yourselves. *Ná mín avaskathí*. May no evil come to you." He handed Nancy a set of car keys, saying he would be back in a week.

The streets of Athens were congested with private cars and taxis which honked and weaved in front of one another, sometimes dangerously close. Nancy gripped the steering wheel tightly as she drove to the outskirts of the city. There the narrow roads opened onto a highway. She followed it to Piraeus, the busiest port in Greece.

"There it is!" George exclaimed, spying a gray building with the name NIKOS across the top.

Inside, Nancy asked for Helen's cousin, Constantine. She was not surprised to learn he no longer worked there.

"Do you know where he is?" Nancy asked, looking at the man squarely.

"No. Constantine is a wild boy with wild friends. He spent all the money his parents left him, then—poof!—like smoke—he disappeared!"

"What about the lawyer, Mr. Vatis?" Nancy probed.

"Out of business."

George muttered, "I have a feeling we River Heights detectives are out of business, too!"

"Not yet, I hope," Nancy said. She asked the man for permission to board one of the Nikos freighters. He gave her three passes and, to her bewilderment, a snapshot of a handsome young man.

"Constantine," he said with a nod. "You may keep it."

"He looks like Helen, don't you think?" Bess commented, observing the soft brown eyes and wavy hair.

"A little," Nancy agreed. She stowed the picture in her purse and noted the man's directions to a freighter berthed near the shipyard.

"Someone will let you on board," he said. "I hope you enjoy your visit and your vacation in our country." The girls thanked him and left.

"What do you figure we'll find?" George asked.

"Some cute sailors," Bess answered, dimpling.

"Or a few Greek rats!" George quipped.

Her cousin shivered as she eyed the large gray tanker in front of them.

"Well, let's go aboard," Nancy urged, and the girls walked up the gangplank.

They gave their passes to a crewman who spoke to them in Greek.

"Here we go again," George sighed. "Does anyone speak English here?" she asked him.

The man stared at her. He shrugged and walked away, leaving the visitors to explore the ship alone. They stepped below deck. Suddenly the freighter began to move.

"Where are they taking us?" Bess cried.

5

In the Ditch

The young detectives raced upstairs. Already the freighter had slipped a few feet out of its tight berth.

"Stop!" Nancy shouted to a crewman while George and Bess waved their arms frantically toward the dock.

"Let us off!" they exclaimed.

The crewman jabbered back in Greek, then yelled to another man who bolted through an iron door.

"What'll we do if the boat keeps going?" Bess said anxiously.

"Jump overboard and swim back," George teased.

"Won't be necessary," Nancy said. "We're going back!"

"Phew!" Bess exclaimed. "That was a close call. We could've been kidnapped—"

"And left to die on some sinking island!" her cousin said as the girls stepped onto the dock.

"Tomorrow we'll do something a little less eventful, okay?" Nancy said, and suggested a visit to Maria Papadapoulos's home.

"Does her family know we're coming?" George asked on the way there.

"Not unless Mrs. Thompson wrote to Mrs. Papadapoulos. Anyway, she gave me a letter of introduction to bring along."

The car rolled on smoothly for several miles, passing groves of olive trees along a highway that curved along the Canal of Corinth. When they reached the hillside village, Nancy shifted to low gear on a steep incline. For a moment she dropped her gaze, unaware that a small pickup truck was speeding down the narrow curve toward them.

"Oh, no!" George cried in alarm.

The truck was gaining speed. In a few moments the two vehicles would collide! There were no side roads or driveways to escape into, only a deep, muddy ditch!

"Hang on!" Nancy told the others, steering sharply to the right out of the truck's path.

The car bucked into the ditch like a bronco. Its rear wheels kicked high as the front ones spun forward in the dry mud, spewing it in all directions, before the vehicle finally came to a complete halt.

Nancy let go of the wheel and sank back against the seat. "That was a close one!" she exclaimed. "Are you all right?"

"Uh—okay," Bess said weakly.

George grinned. "I feel like a cowgirl, and glad this animal has stopped! How about you, Nancy?"

"I'm okay." Actually, her hands and arms ached from clenching the wheel so tightly. She took a deep breath and said, "Let's try to push the car out."

"We'll never be able to budge it," Bess predicted.

"Where's the old positive thinking?" George said brightly, and anchored herself behind the right rear bumper. "Ready?" She glanced at Nancy, who stood in a similar position on the left side.

"Ready!"

Bess lined herself between them. "One, two, three, push!" she said. But the car did not move. "Is the brake off?"

"Yes," Nancy puffed. "Let's try again. Two, three, push!"

This time the car slipped ahead, but not far.

"It's useless!" Bess declared, collapsing on the trunk.

George rested against it, too, while Nancy walked to the front. The wheels were choked with mud.

"What we need is a crane," she sighed.

In the distance, a stout woman in an old cotton dress emerged from a small farmhouse. With her were several children who hung close to her as she hurried toward the girls. She chattered at them in Greek, and looked piteously at the car.

"*Parakaló*, just a minute, please," Nancy said, reading the small Greek-English dictionary she took from her purse. Quickly she flipped through it, picking out *voíthia*, *autokínito*, and *mihanikó*, which meant "help," "car," and "mechanic."

The woman nodded with understanding and patted one of the children, saying, "Zoe! *Grígora! Grígora!*"

"That must mean 'Hurry,' " Bess whispered to Nancy.

"*Fére tón Babá!*" the woman continued.

Shortly, the little girl returned with her father, a man not much taller than his wife but as muscular as she was plump. He circled the car quickly, then got inside and started it, pressing the gas pedal to the floor. The others stood back as mud churned under the racing wheels. Suddenly, the car lurched forward.

"*Efharistó*, *efharistó*, thank you," Nancy said when the car stood on the road once again.

The couple smiled happily as the girls gave each child a shiny American coin. They grinned and waved good-bye to the travelers who set off for the Papadapoulos home, a small stone house down the road.

"Welcome," Mrs. Papadapoulos greeted them. She was a slender, dark-haired woman with a pale face. A little girl with huge dark eyes clung to her skirt.

Nancy handed her Jeannette Thompson's letter of introduction.

"Cannot read," the woman said. "Maria, you—"

Her daughter, who was nine or ten years old, spoke. "Mama knows only a few English words."

"But you speak very well," George remarked.

"That's because I went to school in Athens."

Maria glanced at the letter and seeing Mrs. Thompson's name at the end of it, she grinned. "She is a nice lady. She helped us a lot, but she stopped."

As she talked, her listeners looked past her at the rugs and afghans handwoven with red and brown wool. They were a striking contrast against the pure white cotton cloths trimmed in needlepoint that hung over the tables and chairs.

"Mrs. Thompson never stopped helping you," Nancy assured her. "Somebody stole the money!"

Maria gasped and sputtered in Greek to her mother, who looked equally shocked. Her eyes brimmed with tears which subsided only when

George asked to see some of her handiwork. Quickly Maria brought a cloth bag. Her mother opened it and pulled out a beautifully embroidered shawl.

"How lovely!" Bess murmured. "Is it for sale, Maria?"

The little girl repeated the question in Greek. Mrs. Papadapoulos shook her head. "A gift," she said, wiping her eyes.

"That is very kind of you," Bess said sweetly, "but I can't take it unless I pay for the shawl. It's not for me. I want to give it to someone else."

When Maria explained to her mother, she reluctantly accepted a small sum of money. Then, digging back into the bag, she produced a pretty white handkerchief with an unusual lace edging. She handed it to Bess. "For you," she said. Pulling out two more, she gave them to Nancy and George.

"*Efharistó*," the girls answered gratefully.

"I suppose," Maria said, "Mrs. Thompson will not want to—"

"When she got your mother's letter, she was very upset," Nancy interrupted.

"I wrote it for my mother—"

"Well, she realizes how much you all have depended on her."

Before the girl could continue, the door swung

46

open and two small children, younger than Maria, ran in.

"*Éla, éla.* Michali! Anna!" their mother exclaimed. "Come here, we have guests."

She sent them to fetch glasses of fresh goat's milk for the visitors. Bess swallowed hers quickly.

"It's delicious," she said. "You ought to make goat's milk candy."

"Think so?" Maria giggled. "How much milk would it take? We only have three goats!"

"In that case," Bess said, excusing herself, "I'll be right back." She returned with a large picnic basket filled with delectable food from Athens.

"Where did you hide that?" George asked in amazement.

"In the trunk," Bess replied smugly.

Her friends helped lay out the meal. Despite everyone's hearty appetite, there were plenty of leftovers for the Papadapoulos family.

When the girls were on their way back to Athens, Nancy and George praised Bess extravagantly. "It's the first time you didn't go for second helpings!" George teased. "Now that you've started the diet, how about sticking to it?"

Bess did not retort.

As they drove along an attractive bathing beach, Nancy gazed longingly at a strip of white sand dotted with sunbathers. "If only we had brought our swimsuits," she said with a sigh.

"That's my second surprise," Bess piped up, announcing she had packed everyone's gear. "I was hoping we'd have time for a dip!"

Eagerly Nancy parked the car and Bess removed the beach togs. The girls hurried to the ticket booth and bathhouse. They changed quickly and, after dropping their towels on the coarse sand, ran into the surf. Nancy and George dived under a wave, feeling the cool water tingle against their skin, while Bess began to sidestroke near shore.

"It's wonderful," she thought as the salt water licked her face. Then, changing direction, she let her toes touch bottom. Instantly, she let out a cry of pain!

6

Hunting a Suspect

Hearing Bess's cry, Nancy and George swam toward her from opposite directions. They sliced through the water quickly but were still several feet away when the lifeguard reached her.

"My foot hurts," Bess was saying to him as she limped onto the beach.

The young man knelt to look at the red mark on Bess's skin. "You were stung by a jellyfish," he said, then stood up again. "You'll be all right. I have some—"

"What happened?" George interrupted as she and Nancy caught up to the pair.

Nancy's gaze traveled to the bite. "Do you have any rubbing alcohol?" she asked.

"No," the lifeguard said, "but I have a solution of ammonia."

"Ammonia!" Bess gasped. "Ick!"

The young man ran to a canvas bag next to his chair and removed a bottle of clear fluid. Within seconds he was pouring some of it over the large welt.

"Ou-ouch!" Bess cried out. "That burns. It hurts more than the jellyfish!" She shook her foot vigorously and to her relief the sharpness of the sting abated quickly.

"You see, I told you you'd be all right," the lifeguard grinned. "Alexis is never wrong."

For a long moment Bess returned the smile, dimpling her cheeks as she blinked in the sunlight. "Alexis?" she paused for the rest of his name.

"Hios."

"The shipping family?" Nancy inquired.

"That's right. We're from the island of the same name."

"Then why are you here in Loutraki and not sailing on some gorgeous yacht?" Bess asked.

"I will be on one later this summer. Would you all like to go?" he said hastily.

The sunlight danced on his deeply tanned shoulders, making the visitors wish they had more time to spend on the beaches of Greece.

"I'd love to," Bess replied.

"But we don't plan to stay the whole summer," George put in quickly.

"We're really here on business," Nancy ex-

50

plained. "As a matter of fact, it involves the shipping family of Nicholas, who own the Nikos line."

"Oh, yes. I know them."

"You do?"

"Of course," Alexis said. "The shipping community is a very close-knit one."

"Then maybe you know Constantine Nicholas," George put in. "Do you?"

"Yes."

"Well, we're looking for him. I mean Nancy is."

Alexis seemed somewhat guarded as he went on. "I understand he disappeared with a lot of money, some of it his inheritance from his parents and the rest stolen. It's possible, though, the story is only gossip."

"What else have you heard?" Nancy prodded.

"First, can you tell me why three pretty American girls are so eager to know?"

Briefly, the girl detective mentioned that her father was Helen Nicholas's lawyer and that he had asked Nancy to search for Helen's missing cousin, Constantine. "The stolen money you referred to—was it stolen from Uncle Nicholas's estate?"

"Maybe. I know that the old man hoped Constantine would carry on the business after his death. But now he's gone, and no one knows where."

Alexis could shed no more light on the subject, and the young people began to chat about Greece.

"Have you ever been to Lycabettus Hill?" Alexis inquired.

"Where's that?" Bess asked.

"In Athens," he said. "It has a spectacular view of the city. There's a small church, too, and a restaurant. Maybe you would all like to go there with me this evening."

"Sounds great," George replied.

"Shall we meet about eight thirty?" Nancy said as the girls picked up their beach towels.

"Fine. Just tell me where you're staying," Alexis said.

"The Hotel Skyros," Bess replied, waving goodbye. "See you later."

The young detectives changed into dry clothes and as they were starting back for Athens, Nancy mentioned Mrs. Thompson. "I ought to phone her about our visit to Agionori."

"Forget using the hotel phone," George said. "It takes forever to get through."

Consequently, after Nancy returned the car to the garage, the trio headed for the kiosk near their hotel. Nancy dialed Mrs. Thompson's home telephone number, listening to it ring several times before hanging up, then tried Helen Nicholas. She did not answer.

"Maybe Dad's in," Nancy murmured, making the third call.

To her delight, he picked up the phone immediately, and Nancy related her current news.

Bess, meanwhile, pulled George aside. "Do you see that guy up the street?" she asked.

A tall man with black hair was pacing back and forth in front of an iron fence.

"What about him?" George replied.

"I think he's the one who took the basket of apples from our hotel room!" Bess said.

"Oh?" George said. "Let's watch him."

As soon as Nancy finished her conversation, Bess told her about the suspect. Suddenly she let out a stifled cry.

"And look who else is coming," Nancy remarked.

Approaching the stranger was Isakos, the unpleasant man they had met on their flight to Athens!

"Follow me!" Nancy urged her friends. She led them onto a side street that curved back to the one where the men were standing.

The girls walked briskly toward a profusion of bougainvillea vines entwined around an iron fence and parted the flowers enough to see Isakos's red face. He was moving his lips, but the words were barely audible. Then his voice rose.

"At two or three tomorrow morning no one will be around St. Mark's!" he insisted. "It will be perfect. We can take—"

"Don't speak so loudly!" the other man cautioned him.

"I can't hear everything they're saying," Bess whispered to Nancy.

"Sh!" her cousin warned.

They heard only a few more words, including a vague reference to mosaics, before the pair moved down the street. They crossed it, apparently aiming for the Hotel Skyros.

"Do you suppose the men are staying there?" Bess asked, following her cousin and Nancy through the square.

"If not both, then I bet one of them is," Nancy said upon entering the hotel. She stopped at the desk to inquire.

"Why, yes," the clerk answered, "there is a Mr. Isakos in Room 986."

"Thank you very much," Nancy said.

"Do you wish to leave a message?"

"N-no," Nancy replied. The number of the man's room was racing through her mind. Theirs was 968! Had the venomous snake in the basket of apples been meant for Isakos? If so, why?

The same questions occurred to George. "Our room isn't far from 986," she said as they took the elevator to the ninth floor.

When the girls reached it, no one was in the hallway.

"All clear," Bess said, tiptoeing with the others to Isakos's door.

They listened a bit, but heard nothing.

"Maybe the other guy left," George whispered.

"And maybe he's on his way back," Bess pointed out. "We'd better go."

The girls hurried to their room to rest awhile before they showered and changed. Less than an hour before Alexis was due to meet them, Nancy slipped into a pretty turquoise skirt and blouse. Bess put on a white eyelet dress, and George, a tan silk outfit.

When they strolled out of the elevator onto the first floor, they found Alexis seated in a comfortable chair under a palm tree. His deep tan was a striking contrast against his white shirt.

"Hi!" the girls greeted him, prompting the young man to rise.

"I have some news for you," he said mysteriously.

"You do?" Bess asked eagerly.

"I think I saw Constantine."

"Where?" Nancy asked in surprise.

"Near Plaka. I. tried to catch up to him, but couldn't. There were too many people around."

"Maybe Constantine works at the flea market," Nancy said thoughtfully. "We ought to go there in the morning to find out what we can."

The other girls agreed, but as they approached Lycabettus Hill, the conversation quickly changed.

"How do we get up there?" Bess inquired.

"On the funicular," Alexis said, pointing to a cable car ready to ascend through a tunnel. "It will take us to St. George's Church."

"Speaking of St. George's," Nancy said as they boarded one of two compartments, "is there a St. Mark's Church nearby?"

Alexis pondered a minute. "Not that I know of," he said.

"Well, I'm thinking of some place called St. Mark's that may have some unusual icons or mosaics," Nancy went on.

"Oh, yes. The monastery."

"Is it in Athens?"

"No, no. It's on the northern outskirts." As Alexis spoke, the car began to slide through the dark tunnel, breaking slowly away from the buildings below.

"This is fantastic!" George exclaimed when they reached the top of the mountain.

The church was small and white, a stark contrast against the awesome view from the hill. Alexis swept his arm toward the Acropolis, where a rainbow of lights played over the temple ruins, then pointed out the King's Palace and, in another direction, the harbors of Piraeus.

56

"We'd never have come here if we hadn't met you," Bess said to Alexis. "Thank you."

"My pleasure," he answered. "I hope to convince your friends to stay all summer."

The evening wore away quickly and at the end of it, the girls promised to keep in touch with their new friend.

Next morning, the girls awakened early and directly after breakfast went to the jewelry shop in monastiraki.

Nancy's first question to the shopkeeper was, "Do you recall the name of the man who bought the gold mask?"

The woman glanced in bewilderment from Nancy to the other girls. "Gold mask? What gold mask?" she repeated.

"The one you had in your window," Nancy said.

"I don't know what you are taking about."

"Surely you remember all of us," the girl went on.

The shopkeeper remained silent. It was only when Bess decided to purchase a gold filigree bracelet that she smiled a little.

"A very pretty choice. Excuse me while I wrap it."

"Weird," George commented as the woman slipped behind the curtain, but hearing a low murmur of voices, she said no more.

Nancy tiptoed near the curtain. She caught a few Greek words, *símera, ti óra, stís októ, apópse,* and finally the name of the girls' hotel!

"Something's about to happen at the Hotel Skyros!" Nancy gasped.

7

Burglar Attempt

Before Nancy could tell her friends what she had overheard, the curtain was flung back. The shop-keeper appeared, holding Bess's purchase.

"Is there anything else you would like?" she asked the girls.

"No, thank you," George replied, signalling her cousin to leave.

Outside, Nancy opened her Greek-English dictionary, then said, "Something related to the three of us is going to happen at our hotel tonight about eight o'clock!"

"What!" Bess exclaimed.

"But where?" George asked. "We can't cover the entire hotel. There are fourteen floors—"

"And a lobby," Bess interrupted, adding, "Are

you positive the shopkeeper was talking about us?"

"No, I'm not," Nancy said, "but my hunch is yes. Anyway, we should stick around to see what happens."

That evening, the girls strolled through the hotel at the appointed hour. As a precaution, Nancy asked the hotel desk and telephone operator not to reveal the girls' room to anyone. Bess offered to post herself near the busy side entrance.

"Where are you two going to be?" she asked.

Before either could answer, a call came over the loudspeaker for Nancy Drew to answer the phone. "George, will you check that out for me?"

"Sure. Where are you going?"

"Upstairs to our room."

"Alone?" Bess asked fearfully.

"I'll be okay. You stake out the side entrance and don't worry. I have a feeling that phone call is meant to keep us away from our room."

The girl detective took the elevator to the ninth floor. Instinct told her to step out cautiously. As she approached her door, a man suddenly appeared from the stairway exit. In his hand was a key which he inserted in the lock of her room!

"Stop!" she shouted, racing toward him.

He whirled quickly and hurled something in her direction, then dashed to the stairway.

"Stop! Stop!" Nancy cried again, dodging the object. She ran after the intruder, tracking him to the floor below. He dashed into an elevator with a couple who were just entering. The door closed just before Nancy got there.

He's probably going to the lobby! Nancy thought.

Instantly, the girl detective flew back to the stairs, bolting down each flight with amazing speed. Upon reaching the ground floor, she gazed about breathlessly, hoping the man would still be in the lobby. There was no sign either of him or of the couple who had ridden with him.

Nancy hurried to the desk. "*Parakaló,* excuse me," she said. "I'm looking for someone." She described the suspect and the couple and added, "Are they staying in this hotel?"

"I don't recognize the man but the couple sound familiar. They are staying here. Their name is Zimmer. I believe they are members of a charter tour from Massachusetts."

Just then, George spotted Nancy and ran toward her. "That phone call was from a newspaper reporter." she said. "He wants to write an article about you."

"About me?" Nancy said. "Why?"

"It seems he heard you were in Athens to solve a mystery and wishes to know what it's about."

"You didn't tell him, did you?"

"Are you kidding? I wouldn't tell anyone. I said, 'What kind of a detective would I be if I told you over the phone?' "

"And what did he say?"

"He didn't want all the details—just enough to make an interesting story. 'Even so,' I said, 'I really can't help you.' " She paused. "I believe he thought I was you until I slipped and told him I wasn't Nancy Drew."

"Then what happened?"

"He was furious and hung up."

"Did you find out his name?" Nancy inquired.

"Yes, it's Irwin."

"And which paper does he work for?"

"He's a free-lance writer. At least, that's what he said. He claims he's developing a column that focuses on Americans living or visiting in Greece."

"I think," Nancy told George, "that Irwin, if that's his real name, was only trying to keep me from going to our room, while his buddy went in." She told about her ride to the ninth floor and what had happened. "The man looked like the one who took the apples—"

"Where did he get the key?" George asked. "Do you think he works at this hotel?"

"Possibly. Or maybe he stole a master key and had a duplicate made before anyone discovered the original was missing."

"Terrific," George said, shaking her head in concern. "If you're right, then he could return at any time."

"We don't have much of value for him to steal," Nancy said. "What really bothers me is that he can harm us. Apparently, the apples were meant for us after all."

George nodded worriedly. "We'd better change rooms before—"

Just then Bess ran up to them. "Wait until you hear this!" she panted.

"What?" Nancy asked.

"A man ran out of the elevator and almost bumped into me. I heard him say 'Drew.' "

"Why didn't you follow him?" George pressed her cousin.

"I tried to, but he got away from me. He jumped into a car and they took off."

"They?" George asked.

"There was another man behind the wheel."

"Did you notice a couple with them?" Nancy continued.

"Come to think of it, there were two people in the elevator, but they didn't go with him. They looked as mystified as I was when he cut out in front of them. I'm positive the rude one was the man we saw with Isakos!"

Suddenly, Nancy recalled the object he had

hurled at her in the hallway near the girls' room.

"Let's go upstairs," she said. "On the way I'll tell you what happened to me."

When Bess heard about the intruder, she turned pale. "We'll have to move out of here!" she insisted. "What if the guy slips us another poisonous snake?"

"If you would feel safer in another room," Nancy said, "we can arrange it. I'm staying where we are."

"But why expose yourself to danger?"

"What's to prevent him and his pals from finding us in another room? If we leave the hotel, we might lose track of our enemies. I don't want to do that. I want to catch them!"

"Nancy's right," George agreed. "We're a team, and facing the danger is winning half the battle!"

The girls stopped near room 968.

"There it is!" Nancy cried, seeing something that lay on the hallway carpet. She hurried forward and picked it up. "It's a metal stamp," she said.

On the bottom was the strange serpentine symbol that appeared on the gold mask!

8

Valuable Outburst

Were the intruder and Isakos working together as art thieves? Nancy wondered. If so, had one of them planted the mask in her shopping bag, hoping the police would arrest her if she tried to return it?

"This is absolutely incredible," George said, staring at the stamp.

"It must be used to identify all the stuff stolen from the museum," Bess suggested.

But why was the stranger carrying the stamp with him? Why, too, had he thrown it away so carelessly? Was it done in a fit of frustration?

No immediate answers came to the three detectives as they went into their room.

"Maybe we ought to investigate St. Mark's monastery," George said, "It wouldn't surprise me if Isakos and his friend try to steal some of the icons."

"And stamp them with this," George added.

"Uh-huh. I have a feeling we're in for another long night," Bess moaned. "Didn't Isakos say something about two or three in the morning?"

"Why don't we take a nap for a few hours?" Nancy suggested. She removed Mr. Mousiadis's car keys from her purse and put them next to her digital alarm clock. "Seeing these when I wake up will spur me out of bed." She laughed.

None of the girls slept soundly. When they awoke, it was one o'clock.

"All set?" Nancy asked cheerily.

Bess lifted her head from the pillow, then mumbled something and turned over.

"Come on, sleepyhead!" her cousin prodded her.

"Go away," Bess murmured, but forced herself to get up.

Once she dampened her face, Bess was as eager as the others to begin their journey into the hills. But the monotonous drone of the car engine soon made her sleepy again.

"How much farther do we have to go?" Bess asked when they reached the edge of the city.

"Only a few more miles," Nancy replied, stifling a yawn.

Soon she turned the car onto a narrow roadway that twisted between darkened houses and rows of cypress trees that grew more dense as the iron gate of the monastery came into view. A lone candle was burning dimly in a window.

"How do we get in?" Bess whispered. "The gate looks locked."

Nancy pulled the car to a halt and shut off the headlights. "Where there's a will, there's a way," she declared.

Careful not to make any noise, the three sleuths crept out into the moonlight and moved toward the gate.

"We're in luck," Nancy whispered excitedly. "The bolt's broken."

"Maybe someone forced it!" Bess declared.

"Or maybe it's just rusty," her cousin said, helping Nancy swing back the heavy gate.

Quietly they stole across the paved courtyard, glancing at the candlelit window, and hid near a tree. Suddenly a loud wail drew monks from their cells.

"What's going on?" Bess whispered to the others.

She stuck her head out from behind the tree trunk to watch the men scurrying through the chapel doors at the far end of the courtyard.

"Do you want them to see us?" George asked, yanking her cousin back next to her.

"They won't. It's pitch-black," Bess retorted.

"Sh!" Nancy signalled them to stop talking.

She noticed a glow of light dance on and off across the pavement. Perhaps one of the monks had remained in his cell, turned on a lamp for a moment, then shut it off. But to her surprise the light flickered several times. Was it a signal?

The cousins had also noticed it, but kept quiet as a man in a long black robe darted in front of their hiding place. The wailing sound had stopped and the other priests quickly returned to the courtyard, immediately dispersing to their rooms.

"Let's go to the gardens," Nancy said in a low voice.

Bess grasped her friend's arm. "What if they all come out again?" she asked nervously.

"What if, what if," George grumbled. "What if the sky falls down, Chicken Little?"

With a deep frown, Bess stepped away from the old gnarled tree.

"Stand where you are!" a deep voice ordered.

"Oh!" Bess gasped, freezing in fear.

Nancy whirled and found herself facing the grizzly detective who had tried to arrest her at the museum! "Have you been following us?" she asked.

On the way to the monastery, Nancy had noticed a pair of headlights bearing down on her car, but it had whipped past when she parked.

"I—how you say—have had my eye on you all."

"But I didn't tell anyone where we were going," the girl sleuth said.

"Doesn't matter. Your hotel has been very helpful to the police."

"You mean that someone at the Skyros has been reporting our comings and goings to you?" George inquired in disbelief.

The detective ignored the question. "You have no right to be here," he charged. "This is private property."

"We're investigating something," George explained indignantly.

Afraid that Bess, out of fright, might reveal too much, Nancy said quickly, "We have reason to believe that someone is planning to steal things from this monastery. He may be doing it this very minute!"

"Ridiculous!" the detective sneered.

"If you don't believe us," George spoke up impulsively, "we'll show you!"

"We will?" Bess asked in surprise.

In the back of George's mind and Nancy's was the thought that the man in the black robe might have been Isakos or his partner! Nancy glanced at her watch. It was almost 2:30 A.M.

"He went down there," Nancy said, pointing to a stone passageway across the courtyard.

She led the way to a small room. The wooden door was open a crack and George pushed against it gently. Nancy noticed the walls were devoid of any decoration. There was only a simple altar where a monk knelt in prayer. He jerked up suddenly when the door hinge squeaked, but he did not turn around.

"Oh, excuse me," George apologized. She closed the door.

When the group stood once more in the moonlight, the detective chided them severely. "If I catch you doing something like this again, I will have you sent home!"

"But—" Bess muttered.

"Not another word," the man snapped. "Go back to your hotel at once!"

He strode through the iron gate, escorting the girls to their car to make certain they left before he did.

"What a pill!" Bess commented.

"You can say that again," George agreed.

Nancy, on the other hand, kept her thoughts to herself. Disappointed as well as weary, she drove back to Omonia Square, parked the car, then walked across the street into the empty lobby of their hotel. Even the desk clerk was snoring peacefully in a chair.

"First thing in the morning," Bess stated as they reached their room, "I'd like to go back to the jewelry shop in monastiraki—the one we went to before."

"How early?" George asked.

"Oh, seven or eight," Bess teased.

"You two go ahead," Nancy yawned. "I'm going to sleep."

"Not all day, are you?" Her friends giggled, knowing how unlike Nancy that would be.

The next morning, Nancy was the first one up. Despite the fact she had slept only six hours, she was remarkably refreshed. Bess and George also felt a new surge of energy.

"I can't wait to ask that lady the million-dollar question," Bess said mysteriously.

"Which lady and what question?" George asked.

"The lady in the jewelry shop—" her cousin replied, catching herself before saying more.

When the trio entered the shop, two women stood behind the counter. "You buy *more*?" the older one asked, recognizing the girls.

"No, not today, thank you," Bess said, quickly adding, "Is Constantine Nicholas here, by any chance?"

George glanced at Nancy for her reaction.

"He works here, doesn't he?" Nancy put in.

The younger woman flashed her brown eyes at the girl. "He's not—I don't know where he is. What do you want with him?"

"I merely—" Bess started to say.

"And if he should come back," she thundered excitedly, "he belongs to me. You cannot have him!"

Bess was shocked by the implication. "You don't under—"

"I understand—"

Cutting off the reply sharply, the older woman lashed out at her in Greek. Nancy knew it was useless to ask more questions.

"Bess? George?" she said quietly, nodding toward the door. They excused themselves as Constantine's friend stepped angrily behind the curtain.

As the girls turned the corner up the street, they broke into laughter. Bess said, "She thought I was trying to steal her man!"

"In a way," Nancy said, "I'm glad she did. We picked up a lead on Constantine. He will probably stop by that shop sometime."

"So we should go back again, too," George advised, "but without you, Bess."

Her cousin made a face as Nancy spoke. "Isn't it wonderful—we finally found someone who knows Helen Nicholas's cousin!"

9

The Strange Statue

As the three girls continued their stroll, they found themselves at a sidewalk cafe in the middle of Syntagma Square. A soft breeze rustled their hair while they studied a menu.

"*Parakaló*, I'll have a glass of *visináda*," Nancy told the waiter.

"That sounds interesting," Bess said. "*K'ego*, me too."

"*Triá*," George joined in. Then, turning to Nancy, she asked, "What is it?"

The girl shrugged, a mischievous smile on her face. "I don't know, but Helen Nicholas told me to try it sometime. It's supposed to be very popular here."

In a few minutes, the waiter brought a tray of tall glasses filled with sweet cherry soda.

"Ooh, my favorite!" Bess said happily after she finished a long sip.

George, in the meantime, took a notepad from her purse and tore off several pieces of paper.

"What are you doing?" her cousin asked as she watched the girl write a word or two on each sheet.

"I thought we ought to play tic-tac-toe again. It might help us solve our Greek symbol mystery."

So far George had written the words *inheritance*, *Helen*, *Constantine*, and *Dimitri*.

"Don't forget *Isakos*," Bess put in.

"Or *ship*, the *gold mask*, and *symbol*," Nancy added.

On the remaining pieces of paper, George wrote down *Papadapoulos* and *Mrs. Thompson*.

"That's a lot of clues," Bess remarked. She arranged the words in tic-tac-toe fashion, hoping to make sense out of all the connections. "It's no use," she said at last. "They don't fit together."

It was Nancy's turn next. She set her glass of soda near the edge of the table and picked up the piece of paper bearing the name *Constantine*.

"I'll put him here," she said, placing the paper in the right-hand corner of the imaginary block.

"What about *Helen*?" Bess asked, resting her head on her arm.

"In the bottom left corner," Nancy said, then

quickly arranged six other pieces so that the game
board looked like this:

symbol	gold mask	Constantine
ship	inheritance	Dimitri
Helen		Isakos

"Where do the Papadapoulos family and Mrs.
Thompson fit in?" George asked.

"Oh, they're just innocent bystanders," Nancy
replied.

"And what about the blank space in the middle?" Bess pointed.

"Maybe it's an unknown clue," Nancy suggested.

"Or," Bess went on, "you could put your name
in there."

She was about to tear off another piece of paper
from George's pad when a large cat jumped up and
charged across the table without warning.

"Oh!" George exclaimed.

The glasses teetered, then two of them fell over
before the girls could prevent it. Soda spilled on
some of the papers while the rest floated away in
the gusting wind.

Nancy dived after them, instantly catching two.
The others, however, fluttered in the path of a
Greek girl, who retrieved them.

"Here you are," the young woman said pleasantly, handing the papers to her.

"You're Constantine's friend," Nancy said, recognizing her from the jewelry shop.

"That's right, I-I'm very sorry about what happened there," she replied contritely.

As the two walked toward Bess and George, a waiter was mopping up liquid from the table. The cousins gasped to see the young woman again.

"I am Stella Anagnost," she said, introducing herself.

"And I'm Bess Marvin," Bess replied, extending her hand. "This is my cousin, George Fayne."

"And you are?" Stella asked as she glanced at Nancy.

"Nancy Drew." The girl detective's thoughts were focused on Stella's change of attitude. Although Nancy was eager to ask questions, she waited for Stella to speak first.

"Do you know where Constantine is? I mean, have you any idea at all?" the pretty girl said.

"No, we don't," George answered.

"I know he must be in some sort of trouble," Stella said anxiously. "He hasn't been to the shop in a long time and he has stopped calling me. The last time I saw him he acted very strange—"

"Stella!" A man had stopped by their table and addressed the Greek girl angrily. "You have work to do. Come with me!"

Aghast, the young detectives stared at the stranger, who resembled the man they had seen with Isakos. What was Stella's connection with the men? they wondered. He grabbed her arm and dragged her out of the chair.

"Just a few more minutes," she pleaded. "They can help me find Constantine—"

"Stop it, stop such nonsense!" the man exclaimed, forcing her to go with him.

"But Mimi—" Stella spurted. She tried to break away from her captor, but was no match for him.

"Mimi?" Bess repeated, watching the pair disappear into a taxi.

Before the man stepped inside the car, a small silver money clip fell out of his pocket. He did not hear it hit the pavement as he shouted at Stella, jumped in, and was driven away. Nancy raced to retrieve the clip.

"Look at this!" she exclaimed and showed it to her friends. On the back of the money clip were the initials *D.V.* "Mimi is a Greek nickname for Dimitri," Nancy recalled from her study of the Greek dictionary.

"Too bad his initials aren't *D.G.*," George remarked. "Otherwise he might be the missing Mr. Georgiou."

Nancy pocketed the new clue. "When we see Stella again, we can return it to her and get some more information."

"You mean *if* we see her again," George replied. "It looks as if she's mixed up with the wrong kind of people. They may really hurt her if she steps out of line."

"I think her biggest trouble is Constantine," Bess declared. "She's crazy about him."

"Well, since the jewelry shop will be closing in a few minutes," George said, "we may as well hang on to the money clip and do some sightseeing before we miss Athens altogether."

"I agree," Bess said.

"How about going to the Acropolis?" Nancy suggested. She gathered the pieces of paper on which George had written the important clues. "These go into the purse, too."

The rays of the afternoon sun were tongues of fire as the girls began to look for a cab. Each car, it seemed, already had passengers.

"It's getting frightfully hot out here," Bess complained, feeling a trickle of perspiration drain across her neck.

Nancy finally managed to flag down a free cab, which they took. The windows were lowered, allowing hot air to circulate freely as they sped through the crowded streets.

When the cab reached the entrance to the Acropolis, the visitors stepped out to walk the rest of the way. They paid an entrance fee at the gate, then began the long, hard climb. Ahead of them was the Parthenon. Like a crown jewel, the temple stood majestically among the ancient ruins.

"It's fantastic, isn't it?" George said, admiring the tall Doric columns flanked by marble porticoes.

Nancy's gaze traveled to the north side where a magnificent colonnaded hall had once overlooked the old marketplace. "You know, a number of sculptures were taken from here in the early 1800s," she remarked.

"Were they stolen?" Bess asked instantly.

"No, no. Lord Elgin, who was the British ambassador in Turkey at the time, received permission from the government to remove the pieces. Athens was then part of the Turkish Empire."

Bess's expression remained quizzical. "What did Elgin do with the sculptures?" she inquired further.

"He sold them to Great Britain, which in turn placed them in the British Museum in London."

"What a story," George commented. "I understand that more recently other statues were also removed by the Greek government."

"That's right," Nancy said. "Because of pollution and the fact that tourists had started to chip off marble for mementos."

Bess shook her head in disgust as they all collapsed into silence and drew near another set of columns. They heard a low, indistinct murmur that seemed to shift from one column to another.

"I wonder where that's coming from," Bess remarked finally, turning around to catch the view below.

Red-tiled roofs on the houses of the Plaka below clustered like bright color on an artist's palette, hypnotizing her. Then, as Bess turned to join her companions, who had temporarily left her side, she realized the clasp on her purse was loose.

Oh, I hope I didn't lose any money, she thought, and pulled out her wallet to check.

To her surprise, a small boy dashed from behind a column and grabbed it.

"Come back here!" Bess cried out, alerting Nancy and George to the young thief. "He stole my wallet!"

They chased him down the stone steps, sprinting fast over the ragged marble!

10

Surprise Visitors

"Wait for me!" Bess shouted, running behind the other girls.

They were several feet ahead, trying to keep the young thief in sight, but lost him in a crowd of tourists now beginning their ascent. Nancy and George froze to a halt.

"Why did you stop?" Bess panted as she caught up to them.

"He disappeared," Nancy explained.

"Besides," George said, "I'm getting a blister under my heel." She stooped to loosen the strap of her sandal.

"But what about my wallet?" her cousin exclaimed. She broke into tears. "That was all my money!"

"No, it wasn't," George reminded her. "You still

81

have traveler's checks in your suitcase, don't you?"

"I suppose so," Bess said, "but I just cashed one for fifty dollars and that kid took every cent!"

Nancy slipped an arm around Bess's shoulder. "We'll report it to the police," she assured her.

"And if there's anything else you need to buy," George said, "I'll give you the money."

"You will?" Bess smiled appreciatively.

"We both will," Nancy replied.

The girl dried her eyes with a tissue and followed her friends to the bottom of the hill. Almost immediately, they caught a taxi and went to the nearest police station, where Bess explained what had happened.

"I don't know," the captain said, shaking his head. "Your wallet may be lost forever. But we try to find boy. Tell me, was there American money inside?"

"Yes, some," Bess replied. "Why do you ask?"

"Most likely, he will take it to a money exchange. They give better rates than the hotels—more drachmas for the dollar."

"Maybe we can do some investigating on our own," Nancy declared. "How many money exchanges are there in Athens?"

"Oh, quite a few," the captain replied. "But with hundreds, even thousands of tourists here—no one at an exchange would remember boy." The officer frowned slightly and added, "If we catch him, we tell you."

"*Efharistó*," Bess said as everyone turned to leave. "Now what?" she asked Nancy. "I suppose there's no sense trying to check out all the money exchanges."

"True," the girl detective replied, "but I have a hunch the boy probably stopped at one near the Acropolis."

"I think we passed one when we were in the taxi," George said. "It's that way." She pointed toward a narrow street bordered by apartments.

Quickly, Nancy darted to the traffic light. The cousins trailed after her, crossing the intersection and walking briskly to the other side past the buildings. Soon they reached another corner and their destination.

"Look at that line of customers," George remarked.

"Which line?" Bess asked. "There are about five of them."

"Come on," Nancy said, stepping inside.

The room was crammed with people. Several were seated on benches along the wall, but most of them were standing.

The young detectives separated. Bess looked for the small boy who had stolen her wallet while Nancy and George tried to speak to the clerks.

"Excuse me, excuse me," George said as she weaved in front of two people.

"Wait your turn," a woman in line replied.

"But I only want to ask the teller a question."

"Yeah, well, that's all *I* want to do." The woman squeezed close to the person ahead of her. "I've been standing here for almost an hour," she said, "and you'll have to do the same."

George took a deep breath and gazed in Nancy's direction. Somehow, she had managed to reach another teller. But when the girls met in the back of the room, Nancy looked disappointed.

"I guess the captain was right," she said. "They're all too busy counting money to pay attention to faces." Suddenly, she became aware of the fact that Bess was missing. "Hey, where's Bess?"

"She must have left," George said, rising on tiptoe.

Within a few seconds, however, Bess emerged from the crowd. She was holding a small boy by his shirt collar. "Here's the culprit!" she exclaimed with pride.

"Mommy!" the child cried.

"That's not him!" George said.

"Of course it is," her cousin insisted. "The boy who took my wallet has dark brown hair cut short like this, and he was wearing a blue and yellow T-shirt."

"Well, the one I saw had on blue jeans," Nancy

put in. She stared at the boy's blue slacks.

"How can you be so sure they were jeans?" Bess replied.

"I'm a witness," George chimed in. "And Nancy and I were a lot closer to him than you were."

"Where is your mother?" Nancy asked the boy.

"In line. We just came to Athens today."

The girl did not allow him to continue. Obviously, he was not the thief.

"I'm sorry," Bess said sheepishly. "Here." She handed him one of her tissues.

He buried his nose in it for a second, then slipped back into the crowd.

"Let's go," George declared, "before his mother decides to have you deported."

"It was an honest mistake," Bess defended herself.

Without making any further investigation, the trio returned to their hotel, where they found a message waiting for them. It was written on hotel stationery.

Nancy read it aloud. " 'Surprise! We checked in here today. Give us a call at 1110.' "

"Uh-oh," Bess said. "Don't fall for it."

"There's no signature," George commented as she looked over Nancy's shoulder.

Only a room number," Nancy said. "Maybe it's a ruse to trap us."

"Count me out," Bess said quickly. "There's

85

probably a bushel of apples and snakes waiting for us!"

"I hardly think so," her cousin said. "After all—"

"Even if I'm wrong, I vote to ignore the message completely."

"What if it's from Dave?" Nancy teased. Dave Evans was a special friend of Bess's.

"In that case—" Bess started to say. "But on second thought—"

"Look, why don't you stay in our room while we check out 1110?" Nancy interrupted. "If we don't come back within a reasonable amount of time, send a search party."

"Good idea," her friend agreed.

Bess stepped off the elevator on the ninth floor, leaving her friends to continue to the eleventh. It was still early evening. Several people passed Nancy and George in the hallway, but they recognized no one. Despite the knowledge they were not alone, the girl detectives cautiously approached the door marked 1110. The sound of bouzouki music from a radio floated toward them. Nancy glanced at George and pressed the buzzer.

Soon the door clicked open and two mocha-brown eyes stared at Nancy!

11

Clue on the Dock

"Helen Nicholas!" Nancy exclaimed in surprise and hugged her friend.

"And Mrs. Thompson!" George cried happily when she saw the other woman in the room. "We're so glad to see you! When did you arrive?"

"Just a little while ago," Helen replied with a smile. "I have missed Greece so much. Where's Bess?"

"In our room. I'll call her right away." Nancy dialed their number and invited her friend to join everyone.

When Bess saw Helen and Mrs. Thompson, she giggled. "And here I thought you were kidnappers!"

"Kidnappers!" the women chorused and Helen asked, "Has somebody threatened you girls?"

"Not exactly," George answered.

"We'll tell you everything that's happened so far," Nancy promised, "after you give us your news and tell us what's behind this surprise visit."

"Yes, what made you decide to come?" Bess asked.

"Mostly hearing Helen talk so fondly about the time she spent here as a child," Mrs. Thompson replied. "I just felt I had to see Greece myself. Of course, I dearly want to meet Mrs. Papadapoulos and her children, especially Maria."

"It also occurred to us we might arrange to import some of her handmade embroidery," Helen said.

"That's a fantastic idea!" Nancy exclaimed.

"Helen has agreed to be my interpreter," Mrs. Thompson explained. "Without her help, I'm sure all that beautiful embroidery would probably end up being shipped to penguins in Antarctica!"

"Of course, it would brighten up their tuxedos!" George quipped.

Everyone laughed, then Helen changed the subject. "Now tell us about your adventures in Athens."

Nancy explained what had happened to them, mentioning the mysterious clues they had found. Helen and Mrs. Thompson listened transfixed.

"You're in danger," the older woman said. "I'm not sure it's such a good idea for you to stay here."

"Oh, please don't worry," Nancy said gently. "We're used to this sort of adventure. Besides, now that you're here to help us, we'll round up those crooks in no time!"

This made Mrs. Thompson smile. George quickly asked, "Tell us what you two would like to do this evening."

"Ever since I stepped off the plane, I've wanted to go to Herodotus Atticus," Helen replied.

"The big amphitheater near the Acropolis?" Nancy asked.

"That's right. I saw so many wonderful plays there as a child. Euripides' work was always my favorite."

It was decided that everyone would meet in the lobby at 8:30 P.M.

"Does this mean we're going to skip dinner?" George asked, causing a smile to ripple across her cousin's face.

"Haven't you adjusted yet to the fact that everybody in Greece eats late?" Nancy replied. "We're bound to find a restaurant or tavern open near the theater."

As predicted, there was a festive-looking café within a block of their destination. Helen, however, begged her companions to visit the theater first.

"There is nothing playing tonight," she said, "so we won't stay long."

Bess's stomach growled in discontent. Nevertheless, she followed the others to the theater. Although it was closed to the public, Helen spoke to a guard who consented to admit the group.

"Isn't it marvelous?" Helen cried in delight.

She stepped lightly down a stone aisle and paused to gaze at rows of seats that fanned out from the big stage. She motioned the others to join her. George, Mrs. Thompson, and Bess went ahead of Nancy, who stopped to adjust the strap on her sandal. She became aware of two men talking below her in Greek but paid little attention to them until she heard the name Nicholas!

Excitedly, the girl detective hurried down the steps toward Helen. "Did you hear that?" she whispered.

Helen nodded and held up her hands for the others to be quiet. She was trying to overhear the rest of the conversation.

Suddenly, her eyes flashed. "Nancy!" she gasped. "My cousin is hiding in Pireaus!"

"And to think we were just there!" Nancy said.

"I guess it's time for a return trip," George put in.

"But in daylight, please," Bess commented, gazing up at the dark-blue sky.

The next morning, Nancy volunteered to drive everyone to Piraeus. The harbor was filled with ocean-going tankers and freighters that dwarfed the smaller boats.

"Where shall we go first?" Bess asked.

"I suggest," Helen said, "we park the car and just walk around a bit."

"That's fine with me," Nancy agreed.

All of the conversations they overheard were in Greek. Helen listened closely to one or two of them.

"Anything important?" Bess inquired afterward.

"Possibly," Helen replied. "The men over there said the police have been inspecting freight shipments for some stolen ancient vases. Then I heard the name Isakos."

"Isakos!" the girls chorused.

Nancy scooted to the workmen. "What do you know about Mr. Isakos or Constantine Nicholas?" she asked. Helen, who was behind her, translated the question. The men merely shrugged their shoulders.

"They claim they don't know anything," Helen told her.

"But you *heard* them," Nancy said.

Helen repeated the question. This time, however, she spoke at length. The men in turn gave a long answer.

"What did they say?" Nancy asked Helen eagerly when the exchange of words had ended.

"Not much, really. They didn't tell me any more than I overheard originally. Only that the police have been asking them if they knew a man by the name of Isakos. Apparently, no one does."

The group walked on until suddenly George stopped and pointed to something on the wall of the wharf.

"Look at this!" she exclaimed excitedly.

The initials *D.G.* were carved in the wall. Drawn around the letters was the figure of a serpent!

"What's so unusual about that?" Helen asked. "It's only graffiti."

"There are things scribbled all over the place around here," Mrs. Thompson said.

"But this could refer to Dimitri Georgiou," Nancy pointed out.

"Oh, my goodness! Do you really think so?" Helen responded.

"Definitely."

Ahead of the group was a shipwright who was repairing a hole in the hull of a freighter. Nancy hurried forward, mentioning Dimitri Georgiou's name. The man stopped working and nodded.

He knows him! Nancy thought.

He climbed down his ladder and disappeared for a moment, returning in a few moments with a tall, muscular man.

"Dimitrious Georgiakis," the shipwright smiled,

now revealing a prominent space between his upper front teeth.

Nancy and her companions, who stood near her, responded with disappointed faces. Helen told the men they were looking for someone else.

"Will you ask them, too, if this boat goes to the States?" Nancy requested.

"*Óhi*, no," was the answer.

"I wonder," Nancy said, "if the fake artifacts are shipped first to another country like Italy or France before they're sent on to the United States."

"For what purpose?" George asked.

"To protect the identities of the people involved here."

Interrupting their tour of the harbor, the young detectives decided to talk to the local police.

"*Astinomikós tmíma?* Police station?" Nancy asked a passerby.

The old man lifted his feeble arm and spoke in Greek.

"He's telling us how to get there," Helen explained. "It's not far."

"Can we walk?" George asked.

"Yes."

The group found their way easily. Nancy, again with Helen's assistance, spoke to the police officer in charge. She mentioned their search for Constantine Nicholas.

"I know nothing about him," the officer replied.

"Then what have you found out about the art thefts from the museum in Athens?"

"Nothing I am at liberty to reveal. May I ask why you are so interested to know?"

"Nancy is an amateur detective," Helen answered.

"Oh, I see. Well, this case is meant only for professionals to solve."

The remark nettled his listeners, who said little more than good-bye.

"We're not making a whole lot of progress, are we?" Bess remarked as she walked with the others to the car.

"Where could Constantine be?" Helen murmured. "There are so many factories here."

"And ships," Mrs. Thompson added.

"He could be anywhere," Nancy said, turning on the ignition.

The car sputtered as she pressed down on the gas pedal, then stalled. Nancy tried to start it again, but this time there was only a soft click as she turned the key back and forth. The engine was dead.

"There wasn't a thing wrong with this car before," George said.

Had someone tampered with it?

12

The Banded Freighter

Nancy released the hood and peered under it while Helen and the others questioned those nearby. Was anyone seen near their car?

"Nancy, dear, come here a minute." Mrs. Thompson called out.

The girl emerged from under the hood and closed it. Her friends were gathered in front of a small boy.

"Did you see someone?" Nancy asked, squatting on her feet.

"*Óhi, óhi,*"

"Are you sure?"

The boy weakened. "Big man. Very red face. Gray hair. Mean," he said haltingly.

Isakos! Nancy thought. "Where did he go?" she asked.

"Gave me money," the boy went on. "Not tell anyone."

"But you must tell me where he went," Nancy persisted. "He did something very wrong."

Gently, she laid her hand on the boy's shoulder and stood up.

"Over there," he muttered under his breath. He pointed to the dock, adding something else in Greek.

"He thinks the man went aboard the freighter with the big white stripe around its middle," Helen translated.

"To that one?" Nancy asked. She indicated the ship berthed near the wall marked with the snake symbol.

"*Nai.*"

"No?" Mrs. Thompson sighed.

"On the contrary," Nancy smiled. "*Nai* means yes!"

"Shall we get the police?" Bess asked. "Isakos is three times bigger than all of us put together."

"They'll only tell us to stay out of their business," Nancy said. "Why don't we split up and see what we can find out ourselves?"

"Good idea," George said. "Who's going with whom?"

"Perhaps you and Mrs. Thompson could try finding a mechanic to fix the car, while Helen and I investigate the freighter."

"What about me?" Bess asked.

"You post yourself near the dock to watch for overinterested onlookers."

Bess caught sight of a young policewoman approaching. "See you later," she said to her group, hurrying toward the officer.

When Bess reached her, she was already talking with two young sailors, one of whom was Greek and the other a light-haired Scandinavian.

"Excuse me," Bess said, interrupting the conversation.

The fair-complexioned man winked at Bess. "American?" he asked with a lilting accent.

She nodded.

"Swedish, like me?"

"No," blond-haired Bess answered shyly, "at least, not that I know of."

The policewoman, who was not much older than the sailors, stepped forward. "Do you need some help?" she asked.

"Y-yes, I do," Bess said. Thankful the woman spoke English, she drew her away from the men. "I'm looking for three people, Constantine Nicholas, Dimitri Georgiou, and a Mr. Isakos."

"Just a moment," the policewoman replied. She spoke briefly to the sailors.

"Maybe I can help you," the Swedish man said to Bess. "Constantine Nicholas is connected with the Nikos Shipping Company. I work for them myself once in a while."

"Have you seen him recently?"

"The other day. He wanted to send cargo on the White Band freighter."

That's the one the little boy mentioned! Bess thought. "Does he do that frequently?" she asked aloud.

"Yes and no. Several weeks ago he was around here a lot. Then he disappeared. Of course, I move from job to job. One day I'm in Haifa and the next I'm here. Now he's back, too."

As the young man spoke, his dark-haired companion sidled closer to Bess, causing her to ease toward the policewoman. Bess glanced disdainfully at the Greek sailor.

"Where does Mr. Nicholas live? Here or in Athens?" the officer inquired.

"I'm not sure," the Swedish crewman replied. He ran his forefinger along the crest of his nose. "And I doubt that anybody in Piraeus could tell you."

His companion, meanwhile, leaned toward Bess. "What kind perfume you wear?" he asked in halting English.

"Tea rose," the girl said curtly. "I don't think you can buy it here." She looked straight past him to address his friend again. "I've seen a picture of

Mr. Nicholas, but I'm wondering if he has changed his appearance since it was taken."

"Well, he has a beard and mustache now," the Scandinavian replied.

"Oh, he does? I'm glad to know that."

Thinking the policewoman might glean something else useful, Bess gave her the name of the girls' hotel. "Please don't mention it to these men, though," she whispered.

"Don't worry." The young woman laughed. "That one loves to flirt—especially with pretty American girls."

Bess giggled as she ran toward the white-banded freighter. Nancy, Helen, and a policeman were standing on deck. They were talking to a couple of crewmen. Their voices were heard above the girls'.

Sounds like trouble, Bess thought, speeding up the gangplank to the deck.

"Where do you think you're going?" someone shouted at her.

Bess stopped short. "My friends are up there," she said, turning around to face a short, chubby man in work clothes.

His stern eyes traveled to the deck, then back to Bess. He mumbled, nodding her to move on.

"I found out something important," she whispered to George as soon as she was on board.

"Tell me later."

At the moment, the policeman was involved in a heated discussion with one of the ship's officers.

"They say we have no right to be here," Helen explained to the girls. "But the policeman has told them he will arrest every one of them if they don't obey him."

"I just heard him mention Constantine's name," George said.

"He's asking where my cousin is," Helen replied.

To the girls' surprise, the ship's captain now addressed the group in English. "My name is Fotis. Are you friends of Constantine Nicholas?"

Before Nancy could answer, she noticed steely eyes peering at them from the corner of the deckhouse. The man ducked back for a moment. Then, not realizing he was in Nancy's line of vision, he stuck his head into view again.

"Isakos!" she exclaimed, and quickly darted after him.

13

Boat Chase

Breaking away from the group, Nancy raced toward the man. "Mr. Isakos!" she shouted.

"Where are you going?" the ship's captain bellowed at Nancy. He ran after her with Bess, Helen, and the others following.

The girl detective halted at the end of the deck, where thick coils of rope lay between metal crates heaped in front of a lifeboat.

He's gone! she thought as Fotis grabbed her by the shoulder.

"You have no business upsetting my ship like this!" he hissed.

Ignoring the comment, Nancy suddenly caught sight of Isakos's shirt collar.

"There he is!" she exlaimed. "In the lifeboat!"

Before anyone could catch him, though, the burly man leaped out of it, crashing through piles of crates. He dashed to the other side of the deck and vaulted quickly over the railing. Bess and the policeman sped after him while Fotis gripped Nancy's arm.

"Let me go!" she insisted, pulling away abruptly to join her friends. "Can we chase him?" Nancy asked when she saw Isakos fleeing onto a small cabin cruiser.

Shouting to the crew in Greek, the policeman raced toward the gangplank. Helen and the girl detectives followed him, running every step of the way to a patrol boat moored nearby.

"We'll never catch him!" Helen cried as they watched Isakos disappear behind a jetty.

Nancy, too, became tense as their own boat chugged slowly into the harbor, picking up speed only after they passed an incoming barge. They skirted the jetty and found themselves in the open sea with only the shoreline in sight. Could Isakos's small boat have outdistanced theirs so quickly?

Impossible, Nancy thought.

Then she saw it. The boat lay abandoned on the beach.

"There's a trail of footprints," Nancy observed as they pulled close to shore.

"Bess and I will stay with the boat if you and the

officer wish to search for the man," Helen offered.

"We'll be back before you catch any fish!" Nancy called.

The footprints were still wet, making them easy to track. They led to an unmarked road which seemed to be in the middle of nowhere.

"Isakos must've been picked up by a passing car," the policeman concluded.

"Or a waiting one," Nancy said.

When they returned to the patrol boat, she saw the eager expressions on her friends' faces and shook her head.

"No clues? Nothing?" Bess asked, obviously disappointed.

"Zero."

As Nancy spoke, the officer took the cabin cruiser in tow and headed back to the harbor. Shortly, the white-banded freighter came into view. Fotis stood on deck, holding binoculars.

"He's watching us," Bess remarked. "Are we going to board the ship again?"

"I do have some questions for the crew," Nancy replied.

"And I intend to see their cargo," the policeman put in.

To everyone's amazement, Fotis was less irritable, almost compliant, when the group spoke to him the second time. He instructed a crewman to lead them below deck to storerooms that held a variety of crates. Many had olive oil labels, others cotton, and pelts of fur hung in large refrigerators.

Nancy whispered to Helen and Bess. "What better place to hide stolen artifacts—"

"Than in bales of cotton," Bess interrupted.

"Right." Helen grinned.

"What companies import these?" Nancy asked the crewman.

He did not understand English, however, so Helen translated the question. "He doesn't know," she said.

"Has he seen your cousin? And what does he know about Constantine's shipment of cargo?"

Again Helen spoke to the man. "He says he has never heard of my cousin."

"I doubt that very strongly," Bess said. "The sailor on the dock told me Constantine shipped something on this freighter *recently*."

"Then either this man is lying or the person you spoke to was wrong," Nancy replied.

Now the policeman gave orders for two of the crates to be opened. The crewman balked, muttering in Greek. He threw up his arms as if to tell everyone he had just finished packing the boxes.

"I don't care," the policeman said brusquely, slipping from English back into Greek.

Watching every movement the man made, Nancy concentrated on the crates that contained bales of cotton. Was anything else inside? The crewman seemed to struggle unnecessarily with the staples that secured it. Nancy wondered if he was trying to stall.

Finally, though, the top loosened and the policeman wrenched it off. He opened the bale, then quickly dug into the contents, pulling out a cloud of fiber. It dropped gently to the floor.

Nancy sighed in disappointment. "I was almost positive—" she started to say, poking her hand into the cotton. "Is there anything else in the crate?" she asked the policeman.

"No."

"May we check the other crates?"

"He says they are all alike," the officer replied.

As the group returned to the main deck, they found Fotis waiting for them. "Satisfied?" he said with a smirk.

"Not really," Nancy said.

"I told you there was nothing of interest on my boat."

"That's not true," she declared abruptly. "We discovered Mr. Isakos."

"I never heard of the man," Fotis replied in a smooth tone. "But then, many people come on board when the ship is docked. We cannot check everyone."

He promised to keep in touch with the police and to hold Isakos should he appear on the freighter again.

"I'm sure he will," Bess said cynically.

"I think we would all learn more from the oracle at Delphi!" Helen added. "But don't look so sad. You are making good progress, girls."

"You're sweet to say that," Nancy replied as they left the ship. "Actually, I have a hunch that that freighter is deeply involved in a smuggling scheme. The problem is how to prove it."

14

The Vanished Lawyer

As Nancy, Helen, and Bess said good-bye to the policeman at the dock, they noticed Mrs. Thompson and George talking with a man in blue overalls. Next to him was a tow truck.

"Can't the car be fixed here?" Nancy asked anxiously when she reached the others.

"It already has been," Mrs. Thompson smiled. "We were just discussing the fact that someone deliberately tampered with the engine."

Nancy fixed her eyes on the mechanic. "Did you find any clues to the person's identity?" she asked.

"Clues?"

"Yes, a piece of torn clothing or a button, for instance," Nancy replied. The man shook his head and Nancy opened her purse. "How much do I owe you?"

"Already paid," he said.

"Put your money away, dear," Mrs. Thompson added.

"But I don't expect you—" Nancy began.

The woman shut her eyes, not wishing to hear further on the subject. When the mechanic drove off in his truck, she suggested that everyone have lunch.

"Mikrolímano," Nancy suggested. "It's one of the harbors in Piraeus."

"Are we going to fish for our meal?" Bess asked, grinning.

"Not unless you want lobster!"

The drive to Mikrolímano was short. When a string of restaurants next to the harbor came into view, Nancy pulled to a halt.

"That's the one I told you about," Helen said, pointing to a colorful store window displaying freshly caught fish.

Across the street and down a flight of stairs was a table-lined dock that overlooked the shimmering water with boats moored nearby. A number of customers were finishing their lunch when the visitors sat down. To their surprise, instead of menus, the waiter brought a message.

"It is for Miss Drew," he said.

Nancy opened it quickly, wondering how anybody knew she was there. "It's in Greek, Helen," she said, handing it over.

"The note says, 'I understand you are trying to find Mr. Vatis. I used to work in his office. Maybe I can help you,'" Helen translated.

"Amazing!" Bess remarked.

"That he worked for Vatis?" George asked.

"No, that he found Nancy."

The girls glanced down the row of tables, noticing one man seated alone. A napkin was tied around his neck and he was dipping a small chunk of lobster into melted butter.

"That must be the one who sent the note," Nancy concluded. "He looks familiar, but I can't place him exactly."

"Let's talk to him," Helen suggested. The two stood up and walked to the stranger's table.

"Mr. Vatis?" Nancy asked.

He laid down his fork and smiled. "I'm not Mr. Vatis, Miss Drew. I'm not related to him, and I'm glad of it." He gestured for them to sit down in the empty chairs at his table, introducing himself as Peter Scourles.

"Why are you glad you're not related?" Nancy asked.

"I did not approve of the way he handled estates for people. Your father is an attorney, is he not?"

Nancy nodded, perplexed that he knew so much about her.

"Well, then he would understand what I mean," the man replied. "As a matter of fact, the government of Greece was about to investigate Vatis."

"For what reason?" Helen inquired.

"He disappeared with many important papers."

"Where did he go?" Nancy questioned.

"I don't know, but I think he may be hiding on Corfu. I recall he liked to vacation there and mentioned some hotel with a wonderful view of the sea. Unfortunately, I don't know its name."

Nancy glowed with excitement. Maybe she and her friends could fly to Corfu!

"Mr. Scourles," she said, "who told you about me and my father?"

"I heard of you when I lived in your country and more recently, while I worked for Vatis & Vatis. It was there I learned that Carson Drew represented a member of the Nicholas family in the United States. When Vatis left, I was hired by the law firm who took over his office. You came in the other day to ask for Mr. Vatis. I was standing by the reception desk and heard you introduce yourself."

"Why didn't you speak to me then?" Nancy asked.

Scourles shrugged. "I was in a rush and didn't think of Corfu. It occurred to me later."

Nancy and Helen thanked the man and went back to tell the others what they had found out. Bess and George were thrilled. "Let's go to Corfu tomorrow," George urged.

"I hope to," Nancy replied. "You'll go, too,

won't you?" She was looking at Helen and Mrs. Thompson.

"We'd love to," Helen said, "but we think we ought to see the Papadapoulos family."

They discussed plans for the next day, pausing only to order a sumptuous lunch of seafood and Greek salad. The salt air had increased everyone's appetite, so they added fruit for dessert. Soon the afternoon disappeared as quickly as the fleet of small boats anchored in the quay. The Americans returned to their hotel.

"There's a travel agency in the lobby," Nancy said as they stepped inside.

Yawning sleepily, Mrs. Thompson excused herself to go to her room. The others followed Nancy into a small office decorated with attractive posters of Greece.

"There's a wonderful hotel in Corfu. It's called the Cyclades," the agent told the foursome. "Reasonable, too."

"Does it have a great view of the ocean?" George asked.

"From the top floors, yes. From the lower floors, no. The hotel is in the heart of the business district."

"Hmm," Nancy murmured, then asked to see a brochure.

"If you are looking for a magnificent view," the

young woman continued, "these would be better." She pointed to several listings in the booklet.

"How about this one—the Hotel Kephalonia?" Bess suggested. "It looks gorgeous."

Nancy and George agreed wholeheartedly that it did.

Helen sighed. "If only I could go with you," she said, but she could not be dissuaded from making the trip with Mrs. Thompson to see the Papadapoulos family.

The next day, the girl detectives caught a late morning flight to Kérkyra. It took little more than an hour from Athens.

"I see a taxi," George said, after claiming her baggage. "Meet you out front."

"Okay," Nancy replied. When she and Bess collected their bags, they darted after her.

Aside from the parking lot that stretched against a clearing bordered by brush and trees, the landscape was uninteresting. But as the girls' driver weaved into the colorful shopping district, Bess oohed and aahed over the stores.

"No wonder Vatis loves to come here," she said.

Now the car climbed steadily past villas nestled in a hillside, taking the fork that led to a promontory.

"There it is!" Nancy exclaimed when a gleaming white building came into view.

The driver pulled to a halt at the entrance. Since he spoke fairly fluent English, Nancy asked if they might call him for further work.

"Of course," he said and gave his telephone number.

After the girls registered at the desk, Nancy inquired whether Vatis was staying there, too. The clerk merely shook his head.

"Guess we have to make a few phone calls," she told her companions when they were settled in their room. She pulled out the travel brochure and one by one began dialing local numbers. On her third try, Nancy was successful. "Vatis is staying at the Queens Palace!" she announced in delight.

"That would have been my second choice after this hotel," George said as Nancy hung up and placed a call to the taxi driver.

"I don't want to waste another minute," the young detective said eagerly.

"But the beach looks so inviting," Bess replied.

"We can take a dip later," Nancy pointed out. "Don't tell me you want to miss out on all the fun!"

"Me? Never!"

When they reached the Queens Palace, they learned that Vatis was staying in one of the cottages near the main building. They drove to it. Nancy requested their driver wait for them, then the girls walked to the lawyer's cottage.

"Doesn't look as if anyone's home," George remarked as Nancy knocked on the door.

They peered through half-drawn Venetian blinds. Seeing no one, they circled to the back entrance. A band of wet footprints led up from the beach.

"He must've gone swimming, changed, and left," Nancy concluded. "We'll have to come back later."

"I'd rather face him in daylight," Bess objected.

"He's not going to hurt you," George said assuringly. "Besides, there are three of us against one of him!"

Even so, when they returned that evening, Bess continued to feel uneasy. Before their driver finished asking if he should wait for them, she said yes.

"But please park the car up the road out of sight," Nancy added.

George offered to post herself near the road while Nancy and Bess looked through the window of Vatis's cottage. Inside, the light was on and a man moved about nervously. He was of medium height, dark-haired, and wore horn-rimmed glasses. Presently, he took something out of a suitcase, then lifted the telephone receiver. For an instant, the girls caught sight of an object in his hand.

"It looks like a gold cuff bracelet," Nancy whispered to Bess.

"Apparently he's trying to sell it," Bess replied,

overhearing a snatch of conversation which was spoken in English.

"That's right," the man said. "This bracelet was dug up in 1876."

In the pause that followed, Nancy whispered again to Bess. "1876! That's the year the famous archeologist Heinrich Schliemann discovered the gold death mask!"

"The bracelet was probably stolen from the same museum in Athens!" Bess gasped.

A muffled scream and the sound of dragging feet interrupted Nancy's reply. She and Bess swiveled around fast. George was gone!

15

Corfu Snafu

"Where's George?" Bess gasped.

"I don't know," Nancy whispered, completely mystified.

Several yards away, an engine purred, then roared off quickly. Leaving their post in front of Vatis's cottage, Nancy and Bess raced up the road toward their taxi and leaped in.

"Follow that car, please," Nancy implored the driver, and pointed to the pair of taillights that were fast disappearing down the hill. "Our friend has been kidnapped!"

Instantly, the man turned his cab around and lurched forward, rumbling over the rough road and trying hard to catch up to the other car.

"Faster! Faster!" Bess pleaded.

"I'm going to break the springs under my car," the driver yelled over the racing engine.

Ahead of them, the fleeing vehicle swerved onto another road and cut off two cars ready to make the same turn.

"Oh!" Bess gasped fearfully, as the taxi driver pressed hard on the gas pedal, speeding past the car in front of him. "We're going to get creamed!" She shut her eyes tight.

Nancy, on the other hand, kept calm. "He's heading toward that cliff," she said. "Can you overtake him?"

"This taxi is not a racing car, but I'll try," the man replied as the winding road dissolved in a sharp curve. The cab quickly lost momentum, and Nancy sank back against the seat in disappointment.

Bess, however, sat forward. "Where'd it go?" she asked, staring into the darkness.

"It got away," the driver replied. "Shall I turn back?"

"Let's go a little farther," Nancy urged.

The man grumbled but complied. Suddenly, the glow of his headlights fastened on a figure stumbling out of a ditch.

"It's George!" Bess cried, causing the driver to stop. She threw open the rear door of the cab and jumped out, along with Nancy.

"Are you all right?" Nancy asked the girl who staggered dizzily toward them.

"Fine. I'm fine," George said, but her eyes looked glazed. "I fell, that's all."

Bess and Nancy helped her into the taxi. They stared at the slight bruise along her cheekbone.

"Did he hit you?" her cousin questioned.

"No. He motioned for me to get out, but didn't stop fully. I stumbled and rolled into the ditch."

Nancy removed a tissue from her purse and blotted particles of dirt off George's face. "Who was he?" the girl detective asked.

"I have no idea. He was wearing a stocking mask. He said something in Greek, but I didn't understand it. The voice was a little familiar, but—"

"Do you want to go to the hospital?" the driver interrupted.

George shook her head and Nancy said no. "But are you sure?" she asked her friend.

"Positive. Let's go back to the cottage."

To the girls' dismay, Vatis had apparently left. Was George's abduction merely a ruse to lure Nancy and Bess away from the Queens Palace? They went to the main building and inquired if the man had checked out.

"Yes, he did, but he will be back in a few weeks," the clerk replied.

Instantly, Nancy telephoned the local airport. It

was probable, she thought, that Vatis planned to take a night flight back to Athens en route to some other exotic destination.

"What did you find out?" Bess asked when Nancy rejoined her and George.

"The last two planes just left. One for Athens and the other for Cairo."

"In other words, we're stuck in Corfu for the night," George said.

"It's probably just as well, for your sake," Nancy said. "You need to rest."

"We all do," Bess concurred, blinking her eyes sleepily.

Nancy had reserved seats on the first flight out of Corfu to Athens the next morning and, after breakfast, the trio took one last look at the tranquil sea.

"Too bad we have to leave so soon," George remarked.

"It'll be a long time before we come back, I'm sure," Bess sighed. She stepped out onto the velvet green lawn that swept toward the pool and gazed longingly at the beach below.

Nancy followed her, slipping an arm around her shoulders. Her eyes traced the short strip of sand along the water that lapped peacefully against it.

"Hey, look!" Nancy exclaimed suddenly.

Two men had come into view on the rocky precipice at the far end.

"They seem to be arguing," Bess remarked. "I'm pretty sure one of them is Vatis!"

"But who's the other man?" George asked. "My kidnapper?"

"Bess, you call the police," Nancy instructed.

She and George, meanwhile, hurried down to the beach and ran toward the precipice. The second man, whose back was to the girls, stormed away, disappearing quickly below the rocky ledge.

"Too bad we never saw his face," George said.

Nancy nodded. "But I want to talk to Vatis. Let's hurry before he leaves, too!"

Vatis seemed unaware of their presence. He stared, almost dazedly, into the gentle, deep water.

"Mr. Vatis?" Nancy addressed him.

"What do you want?" he barked, jerking around in fright.

"I've been looking for you," the girl detective said. "Or, rather, my father has been."

"Who are you?" the lawyer asked sharply.

"I'm Nancy Drew."

The sound of the name fell on him like a steel hammer. He gritted his teeth. "Leave me alone."

"I'm afraid I can't do that," Nancy said. "Why did you pretend to check out of the Queens Palace Hotel last night?"

"I don't know what you're talking about," Vatis blazed back.

He lunged at Nancy, grabbing her by the arms. She dug her fingers into his wrists to keep from crashing against the jagged stone.

"Let her go!" George demanded.

Vatis shoved Nancy back against her friend and leaped past them.

"Stop!" Nancy cried, ready to tear after him.

To her surprise, something glittery fell out of the man's pocket, tripping her off balance. It was the cuff bracelet he had tried to sell over the telephone. Quickly she snatched it up and looked inside. Stamped on the bracelet was the mysterious Greek symbol!

16

A Capture

Without wasting another moment, Nancy and George bolted over the craggy rocks to the beach on the far side.

"Vatis is getting away!" George exclaimed as Nancy sprinted ahead, clenching the cuff bracelet tightly in her fist.

"We'll catch you—you won't—" the young sleuth shouted haltingly as the man jumped into a small motorboat and sped away.

"What a shame!" George declared, emptying sand from one shoe.

"C'mon!" Nancy cried out and ran back toward the hotel.

By now, Bess was standing on the grassy overhang in full view of her friends. "The police are coming!" she called.

"Did you tell them to go to Vatis's cottage?" Nancy yelled up to her.

"No. Should I have?"

"Yes, and quick!" George replied.

As Bess hurried back into the hotel, Nancy and George leaped up the flight of stone steps that connected the beach with the pool area. Breathing heavily by now, they darted through the dining room and caught up with Bess at the lobby telephone.

"Let's go!" Nancy said, after Bess hung up. She took the girl's hand to hurry her along.

"Where are we going?"

"To the Queens Palace."

"But we don't have a car," Bess countered.

Parked outside, however, was their taxi driver. He greeted them pleasantly.

"All set to leave?" he asked, smiling.

"We can't go to the airport yet," George said. "We're after someone." She jumped into the back seat with her friends.

"Oh, no, not again!" The man groaned.

Nancy's lips parted into a smile. "I'm afraid so. Can you take us back to the cottage at the Queens Palace Hotel?"

The driver nodded reluctantly. He pulled onto the road, gaining speed at a moderate rate. "After that race last night, this car will never last through the summer," he sighed.

"We can't help it if there's a crook loose in Corfu," Bess said.

"You should leave him to the police to catch," the man replied.

After they passed the sign for the Queens Palace Hotel, a police car came into view. The taxi driver released his foot from the gas pedal, allowing the car to slow down.

"They're here already," Bess observed.

"Thank goodness," the driver mumbled in relief.

The girls stepped out quickly. Nancy skirted the police car to talk with one of the officers.

"What's happening?" she asked him.

"You keep back from the house," he ordered. "The man has locked himself inside. He may become violent."

Nancy produced the cuff bracelet and showed the strange marking inside. The young sleuth explained that she and her friends had overheard Vatis describe its value to someone apparently interested in buying it.

"And you say it was stolen from the archeological museum in Athens?" the policeman questioned.

"That's what I suspect."

A second officer, meanwhile, was shouting in Greek through the cottage door. He ordered Vatis to open it, but the man refused. Through the partially drawn blinds, the policeman watched Vatis frantically empty his pockets.

125

"It's gone! It's gone!" he grumbled to himself. "Those girls must have it!"

He lit a match, dropping it into a metal waste-basket filled with papers. Seeing smoke drift under the door, Nancy ran forward.

"He'll suffocate," she said as the police officer pulled her back. His colleague, meanwhile, smashed the window with a wooden club, tore down the blinds, and climbed inside.

Smoke billowed out and Vatis coughed as he gasped for air. While one policeman snapped handcuffs on him, the other one doused the fire. It had destroyed most of the papers. As the trio emerged from the cottage, Vatis glared at Nancy.

"Give me that bracelet," he growled. "It's mine. It was payment for legal services."

"From whom? Constantine Nicholas?" Nancy replied with equal confidence. "You were blackmailing him, weren't you?"

The man's eyes did not shift from hers as she went on. "You knew Constantine was mixed up with art smugglers and when he couldn't pay you for your work, you accepted this bracelet instead."

"Except," Bess added, "Constantine didn't know that Vatis was stealing the inheritance from him and Helen."

"Precisely," Nancy said.

Despite the accusations, the man did not seem bothered. He gave a self-satisfied grin.

"I will get the smartest lawyers in Greece to defend me. They will prove my innocence," he boasted.

The policemen, in the meantime, took custody of the stolen bracelet. "Someone else will be sent to investigate the cottage thoroughly," one officer said as they went off with their prisoner.

"We ought to check this place right now," Nancy said.

"But we won't be able to remove anything," George reminded her.

"No need to," Nancy put in. She took a small camera from her shoulder bag. "I was planning to take pictures before we left the hotel."

The young detectives went quickly to the wastebasket and examined the burnt papers. There were several readable fragments which Nancy photographed. Her camera automatically produced small color prints.

"We can have these enlarged later," she said, sticking them in her purse. "Right now, let's try to catch our flight to Athens."

The girls rode back to their hotel, asking their driver to wait for them. "We'll be out in a sec—" Bess said as they dashed inside.

The travelers reappeared with their luggage in less than fifteen minutes.

"Do you always rush everywhere you go?" the man asked, breaking into a laugh.

"Not always," Nancy said with a smile. "This really has been a most unusual two days."

In spite of the unexpected delays that morning, they reached the airport with time to spare.

"I don't believe it," Bess kept saying on the plane.

"What don't you believe?" George asked.

"That we solved part of the mystery."

Her remark prompted Nancy to pull out the photographs she had taken earlier. She studied them closely but could decipher only certain initials and parts of addresses.

"As soon as we get into Athens," she said, "I'm going to call Dad. He ought to be in his office now."

Even before she unpacked, Nancy placed the call from the hotel. To her delight, it went through with little trouble. She told her father about finding Vatis and the cuff bracelet stamped with the same intriguing symbol used by the art thieves.

"We'll take the first flight we can get reservations on," Mr. Drew said.

"We?" Nancy repeated.

"That's right. I—"

Suddenly the connection was broken.

"Dad? Are you there?" Nancy said. She pressed down on the receiver hook several times but the line was dead. "I wonder who's coming with him?" she thought, puzzled.

17

Nikos Deposits

"Maybe Hannah is coming with your father," Bess suggested.

"I doubt it," her cousin replied. "I think it's someone from his office."

"Don't you have any idea, Nancy?" Bess asked.

The girl shook her head and excused herself to take a shower. Secretly, she hoped the mystery traveler would be Ned.

"I ought to call Helen and Mrs. Thompson," Nancy said when she reappeared. "George, would you do me a big favor and take these photos to the camera shop on the corner?"

"At your service."

"Ask them to make enlargements as quickly as possible."

George left, and when she returned, her face was beaming. "They'll be ready tonight," she announced.

"Wonderful," Nancy said.

After dinner, the girls picked up the order and joined Helen and Mrs. Thompson in their room. Eagerly, they took turns telling about their visit with Mrs. Papadapoulos and her children.

"She has agreed to sew lots of beautiful things which we will sell in America!" Mrs. Thompson declared happily.

"That's great!" Bess said while Nancy produced one of the enlarged photographs for Helen to look at.

"Incredible!" the woman exclaimed, staring at it. "This is my uncle's will!"

"No wonder I couldn't read it." Nancy chuckled. "It's all in Greek!"

Helen Nicholas scanned the picture closely. "Apparently, he owned various companies, not just the shipping line," she said. "His interests were vast." She leaned back in her chair, fanning herself with the photograph. "And to think so much of this will now be mine."

"What do you suppose happened to the holdings other than those of the shipping company?" Bess asked.

"I have no idea."

"Perhaps Vatis acquired them somehow," Nancy suggested, "and sold them."

"But how?" Mrs. Thompson wanted to know.

"If the lawyer had access to Mr. Nicholas's papers, he could have forged Constantine's signature." Nancy paused, adding, "Tomorrow we'll try to find out where Lineos Nicholas kept his bank accounts. All right?"

Helen looked soberly at the girl. "All right," she said at last.

The next day, Nancy and Helen made a list of all the banks in Athens. They went from one to the other asking if Lineos Nicholas had maintained an account there.

"I'm getting so tired," Helen said as she pushed open the door of the fifth bank. "Can't we continue this tomorrow?" she begged.

"Tomorrow may be too late," Nancy replied.

"Too late for what?"

"For you. If Vatis was in cahoots with somebody here in Athens, they may know he's been arrested and try to steal the rest of your inheritance."

"Isn't it more likely the two of them would keep a low profile?" Helen retorted.

"Not if they want the money!"

"Well, there's no point debating about it," Helen said. "Where is the next bank located?"

"Not far from here," Nancy replied.

She indicated a brick building two blocks up the street. They walked to it quickly. Inside, a guard greeted them. Helen spoke to him in Greek, and to her delight, he said he remembered her uncle well. He had been sorry when he'd heard that Lineos Nicholas had died.

"Such a nice man," the guard added.

"Did he have a safe-deposit box here?" Helen inquired.

"As a matter of fact, yes. I've been wondering why no one has come to claim the contents."

"Have the bank charges been paid regularly?" Nancy asked, prompting Helen to translate the questions into Greek.

"*Nai*. Yes, at least, so far as I know."

"When is the next billing due?" Nancy asked.

"Tomorrow."

"Wonderful," Nancy said. She snapped her fingers as she and Helen left the building. "You and Mrs. Thompson must come here first thing in the morning."

"To pay for the use of the box?"

"No—to wait for the person who will."

"But how do you know the payment won't be mailed?"

"I don't, but it's worth being here to find out."

As the girl detective recommended, Helen and Mrs. Thompson left for the bank early the following day. The others remained at the hotel hoping for another message from Mr. Drew.

"There's a beautiful embroidered dress in one of the shops downstairs," Bess said, trying to gain the interest of her friends.

"Is there?" George said casually. She helped Nancy swing two chairs out onto the balcony of their room.

"I can see you're both absolutely thrilled about my discovery," Bess murmured as her friends sat down.

"We are," Nancy insisted. But she turned her face toward the shimmering rays of the sun and closed her eyes.

"Are you two going to sit up here all day?" Bess asked impatiently.

"Just until Dad calls," Nancy replied.

"In that case," Bess commented unhappily, "I might as well go shopping alone."

She took the elevator to the first floor and discovered almost immediately that the embroidered outfit was no longer in the window. When she inquired about it, the proprietor said it had been sold the day before.

"Thank you, anyway," Bess said in disappointment.

She took a few moments to look at a selection of pretty needlepoint pillows. Then, as she was about to leave, the dressing-room curtain parted open.

"Stella!" Bess exclaimed.

The other girl did not reply, however. She pretended not to recognize Bess and flew past her out the door of the shop.

"Don't you remember me, Stella?"

Bess trailed after her, but a group of arriving tourists quickly separated the young women.

I wonder why she was shopping in this hotel, of all places, the girl said to herself. Come to think of it, she didn't leave with any packages. Maybe she was in the store when I stepped in and she hid in the dressing room.

Then, suddenly, she saw Stella push open the revolving door of the hotel. The young woman dashed out into the square and hailed a taxi.

I'm just too suspicious for my own good, Bess chided herself. Even so, I'd love to talk to Stella again.

It seemed unlikely that Mr. Drew had telephoned Nancy yet, so Bess did not even bother to tell her friends where she was going.

"Monastiraki, here I come!" Bess decided.

She caught a cab and in a few minutes found herself at the jewelry shop. Strangely, the woman who had waited on her was not there. Instead, there was a completely new staff. Bess asked the man behind the counter for Stella.

"I do not know her," he said pleasantly.

"I'm also looking for Constantine Nicholas."

Again the man shrugged. "Perhaps Mrs. Koukoulis knew both of those people. But—uh—she sold the business to me rather quickly and I am not yet familiar with her customers."

"Or former employees?"

"They're all gone."

Very strange, Bess thought as she said good-bye.

By the time she reached the hotel and the girls' room, Helen and Mrs. Thompson had also returned.

"Where have you been?" George asked. She eyed her cousin's empty hands. "No dress?"

Bess shook her head and related her encounter with Stella Anagnost.

"I also have news," Helen remarked. "A boy brought an envelope to the guard at the bank. It contained the payment for Uncle Lineos's safe-deposit box—"

"Your hunch was right, Nancy," Mrs. Thompson interrupted.

"We asked the boy who he was," Helen said, "but he wouldn't give us his name."

"He did admit, however, that someone from the shipyards asked him to make the delivery," Mrs. Thompson explained. "The man told him to say it was from Constantine Nicholas, who couldn't come himself—"

135

"Because he is living in a monastery outside Athens," Helen concluded.

"Incredible!" George exclaimed.

"The question is, which monastery," Nancy said.

"It's Ayiou Markou," Helen put in.

"St. Mark's—the one we tried to investigate before!" Nancy exclaimed in excitement. "We'll go there tomorrow."

"Why not today?" Bess asked.

"Because Dad's going to be arriving with three big surprises!"

18

Barrel Trap

"*Three* surprises?" Bess repeated. "What are they?"

"If I told you, they wouldn't be surprises anymore." Nancy grinned, saying her father had phoned earlier.

That evening, when Mr. Drew knocked on the girls' hotel door, Nancy opened it with anticipation.

"Ned!" she cried happily.

"Hi!" he said, giving her a kiss.

"Hello, dear," Mr. Drew added from behind.

"Dad, I'm so glad you're here," Nancy said as Burt Eddleton and Dave Evans also poked their heads around the door.

"May we join the reunion?" Dave grinned.

"Can you!" Bess giggled gleefully.

"We had no idea you were coming to Greece!" George said to Burt.

"We didn't, either!" her Emerson College friend replied.

"What I want to find out," Ned said, "is why you went ahead and captured Mr. Vatis before we got here."

Nancy chuckled. "We'll make up for it."

"How?" Bess piped up.

"By giving us three crooks to catch—one per couple!" Nancy said.

"We could go into partnership," George declared. "I have the perfect name for our company—the Sleuth Snoops!"

Everyone laughed, then quickly became serious as Nancy related everything that had developed since Vatis's arrest.

"This photograph is wonderful," Mr. Drew complimented his daughter. He was gazing at the enlargement of Uncle Nicholas's will. "Perhaps Helen and I ought to pay a visit to Mr. Vatis."

"That's fine with me," Helen said.

She smiled at the attorney, who responded with equal warmth in his eyes. Nancy glanced from one to the other.

"Dad, should I go, too?" she asked, trying to suppress a feeling that she might be an intruder.

"No, dear, that won't be necessary," her father answered.

"In that case," George said, "the rest of us can tackle the monastery."

Mrs. Thompson cleared her throat to be heard. "If you don't mind, I'd like to take the time to do some shopping for Maria and the other Papadapoulos children."

"We don't mind a bit," Bess said, slipping her arm into Dave's. "The Sleuth Snoops can take care of the job!"

As planned, the six young people set off for St. Mark's monastery the next day. It was unusually hot and the fact that the air conditioner in Mr. Mousiadis's car was not working did not help. The moment they pulled into the courtyard of St. Mark's, Bess and Dave stepped out and headed for the cool stone bench under a large tree.

"Whew!" Bess remarked. "It's hotter 'n peppers."

"You can say that again," her friend said, and rested against the tree trunk, watching the others disappear through the iron gates.

"Aren't you coming?" George called to the couple.

"In a minute," Bess sighed. She was unaware that the foursome had also decided to split up in twos.

George and Burt headed for the gardens behind

139

the chapel while Nancy told Ned about the prayer room across the way.

"I'd like to see it," Ned said, suggesting that Nancy take the lead.

As they strode across the stone yard, a monk scurried out of his room. He brushed past the pair as if they did not exist.

"I guess they're not used to having visitors," Ned chuckled.

"Guess not," Nancy agreed, stepping into the shady corridor at the foot of the stairway.

To the right was the small prayer room. The door was half-open and no one was inside.

"Where does that go?" Ned questioned, glancing toward the end of the passageway where there was a large wooden door.

"I don't recall seeing that the last time I was here," Nancy commented.

"How could you miss it, Miss Detective?"

"It was easy," she said, frowning playfully. "It was two o'clock in the morning!"

She darted ahead and lifted the latch. The door swung open freely. Beyond was a medium-sized room with little in it. Against one wall was a plain wooden bench.

Suddenly, Ned spotted a huge wooden barrel on its side in one corner. "How do you figure that got through this door?" he asked. Both he and Nancy gaped at the enormous cylinder of wood.

"What interests me more," Nancy said, "are those panels of mosaic on that far wall."

From where she and Ned stood, they saw that the mosaics were precast in wooden frames. They looked like paintings whose colors were finely blended.

"It was clever to mount them that way," Nancy said. "They're attached to the wall on brackets so they can be removed easily and hung elsewhere."

"Just like other pictures," Ned agreed, grinning.

"These may be the mosaics I overheard Isakos talking about—"

Before Nancy could finish her sentence, a pair of black-hooded robes were hurled over her and Ned.

"Ned!" she cried out, but her voice was instantly muffled as rope was lashed around her waist, pulling the material down tightly over her head.

Her companion had been taken off guard as well and trussed up. Unseen hands pushed the helpless couple into the big barrel and the lid was fastened in place.

We've got to get out of here! Nancy thought with determination.

She kicked against the floor of the barrel, rolling into Ned, who struggled to free his arms from the rope that imprisoned him. His movements loosened his bonds slightly and he tried to speak.

"Are you all right?" he asked, gagging on a fold of the black material.

Nancy groaned in reply, if only to let him know she had not fainted from the heat and stuffiness.

If we don't get out of here soon, she thought weakly, I probably will pass out. Ned, too. Please, somebody, help us!"

As if she had been heard, Bess and Dave had begun to search for the couple. "Nancy? Ned?" Dave called several times.

"Maybe they're in the garden," Bess suggested.

At the same moment, the monk who had nearly bumped into Nancy and Ned emerged from the chapel at the end of the yard.

"May I help you?" he asked in English.

There was a gentleness in his voice that immediately calmed the young detectives.

"I hope so," Bess said respectfully. She described her missing friends.

"As a matter of fact, I do remember them," the man said. "I was in such a hurry I almost stumbled into them." He laughed lightly. "I shall have to do penance for that."

"Where did they go?" Dave questioned with growing impatience.

"I don't really know, but why not start by looking over there?" He pointed to the crumbling stairway.

"Good idea," Bess said, murmuring to herself. "Nancy probably would want to visit that little prayer room in daylight."

142

To her chagrin, it was completely empty.

"But there's another one," the kindly monk said, indicating the far door.

Bess and Dave ran ahead, pushing it open with gusto. The large barrel was rocking against the wall and voices groaned inside.

"Nancy! Ned!" Dave shouted, tearing off the wooden lid.

The couple was weak from the heat. They slid limply out onto the floor and lay still as their friends removed the stifling robes.

"Oh!" Nancy said, as she suddenly felt several degrees cooler. She swayed to her feet with Ned's help. He slipped his arm around her waist and led her to the bench.

"Thank goodness you found us," Ned told the others.

The monk, in the meantime, was staring at the wall ahead. "What happened to the mosaics?" he gasped.

Nancy and Ned turned to look. The panels were gone!

"What was up there?" Bess asked.

"Beautiful mosaics," Nancy said incredulously. "They must have been stolen—"

"By the people who forced us into that barrel!" Ned deduced.

"And I know who they are!" Nancy declared.

19

Mosaic Lead

"You know who stole the mosaics?" Ned asked Nancy in surprise.

"Let's say it's a hunch," she replied. Turning to the monk, she asked, "Do you happen to know a man named Constantine Nicholas?"

"Yes, but you don't think he's responsible for this?" he said, motioning toward the blank wall. "It doesn't seem likely. He has been here often, begging for help."

"Help?" Nancy repeated.

"He admitted he was in trouble. He tried to get out of it but couldn't. Whenever visitors appeared, he would put on one of our robes and pretend he was deaf."

Ned leaned close to Nancy. "Doesn't that sound

as if Constantine's the smuggler we're after?" he whispered.

The girl detective nodded, which prompted the monk to ask her, "How well do you know Constantine Nicholas?"

"I've never met him," Nancy said and briefly explained her mission.

A perplexed expression crept into the man's face. Finally he spoke. "I don't know whether the person who comes here is the one you are looking for. In any case, I will have to notify the police about the theft of our mosaics."

"I understand," Nancy said. "But we'll try to find them for you, anyway."

As the foursome emerged into the courtyard again, Burt and George waved to them excitedly. They were standing near the shrub-lined access to the gardens.

"What's up?" Dave asked Burt.

"Follow us," George said mysteriously.

Nancy walked briskly along the stone path that led to a landscaped terrace trimmed with zakinthos, white flowers that closely resembled snapdragons. Beyond them was a clump of olive trees. A man was walking slowly between them.

"Who is it?" Bess whispered.

Nancy trained her eyes on the man, who looked like the man in the snapshot in her purse. "It may

146

be Constantine," she said. "Wait for me."

As Nancy stepped nearer to the man, she noticed the grass was thick and moist.

If he tries to escape, she thought, he won't get far.

She skirted the trees, calling out, "Constantine Nicholas!"

Her heart pounded as she waited for a response. None came, so she repeated the name.

He probably hopes I'll give up and go away, she thought.

To her surprise, the man halted. He stood quietly for several moments, then turned to face the girl.

"You *are* Constantine!" she said as a wave of recognition passed between the two.

"And you are Nancy Drew?"

"Yes, but how did you know?"

"I've seen your picture in the American newspapers."

"I have seen yours, too," Nancy admitted, pulling it out of her purse.

Constantine's sad expression changed only slightly. "It's no use anymore," he said. "I'm glad you found me."

The relief in his voice made Nancy feel that before her was not a hardened criminal but a mixed-up young man.

"I'll pay back everything with the money I'm going to inherit," Constantine said. "That is, if I can find the lawyer who took it and the bracelet I gave him."

Nancy gasped in surprise. She waited until the others had joined them and everyone was introduced before she asked, "You mean you never received your inheritance?"

Constantine shook his head. "I had no money to pay Mr. Vatis for the work he did on my uncle's will, so I gave him the bracelet. Shortly after that, I tried to contact him, but he had moved. I never heard from him again."

"He's in jail," George said. "I suppose we'll be able to find out from him whether your story and his match."

"Oh, I'm so glad someone caught him," the young man replied. "At least—" But his voice broke and he lowered his eyes unhappily.

"Were you involved in smuggling art treasures out of Greece?" Nancy questioned.

Constantine nodded.

"Is that how you got the bracelet?"

"Yes."

"And you planted the gold mask in my shopping bag. Why?"

"Yes, I did. The store was—what you call—a 'drop' for things stolen from the archeological mu-

148

seum before they were shipped abroad." He took a deep breath before continuing. "I wanted to return the mask. I couldn't do it myself but I figured that a smart American girl like you would find out where it belonged."

"But Nancy almost got arrested for doing so," Bess informed the young man.

He furrowed his eyebrows in bewilderment.

"They thought Nancy was part of your gang," George explained.

"How terrible!" he said. "That was not my intention at all."

"What was the purpose of stamping that symbol on the mask and the bracelet?" Nancy pressed on.

"It was a way to identify and separate the real artifacts from the fake ones which were being shipped to America as exhibits. I'm surprised you noticed the symbol."

"Was it your idea?" Nancy asked.

"No."

"Was it Isakos's?"

"No. I don't know who thought of it."

"Were the artifacts shipped on the white banded freighter?" George spoke up.

"Yes, but I don't know much about that part of the business."

"Your cousin Helen is here in Athens looking for you," Bess put in.

"And Mr. Drew is trying to settle the inheritance for her," George added. "He needs your help."

"I will do whatever I can," Constantine responded. "Where is Helen staying? Can you bring her here?"

"More likely we will be taking her to visit you in jail," Burt said.

Constantine nodded. "I know. But please let me stay here just a little longer. I'm safer here than I'd ever be in jail, and I need to speak with the monks."

Just then, the holy man who had helped rescue Nancy and Ned approached the group. "It is all right," he assured them all. "Constantine will not escape. We will watch him."

"Thank you." Nancy smiled at him.

The young people said good-bye and left the monastery. The drive back to Athens was filled with speculation about how the other smugglers could be caught.

"It seems to me," Ned said, "if we can round up the key people, the police ought to be able to catch the rest."

"I'm glad we found Constantine, at least," Bess commented as she gazed out the car window. "He's really cute."

"You think so?" Dave asked instantly.

"Yes, very. Dark hair, dark eyes—"

"Each to his own taste," Ned cut in as he swung the car toward a major intersection.

Suddenly, Nancy stuck her head out the open window on her side. "Stop the car, Ned! Let me out!" she cried, and unlocked the door.

He grabbed her arm before she dived into the moving traffic.

"What's going on?" Bess asked.

"I just saw Isakos again!" Nancy exclaimed.

Ned pulled the car to a halt and released his grip on Nancy. She flung open the door and raced after the burly man.

"Isakos!" she shouted, dashing across the street.

He turned, poised on the edge of the curb.

"This is the last time you will bother me!" he snarled. When she was within reach he lunged forward and shoved her back into the heavy, oncoming traffic. Car brakes squealed as Nancy tumbled into their midst!

20

Smugglers' Arrest

"Nancy!" a voice cried as she barely missed being struck by an oncoming car.

It was Ned. He ran in front of the vehicle, causing it to jolt to a stop.

"Ned, Ned—" Nancy murmured. With his help, she stumbled to her feet.

The driver of the car shouted angrily at the couple, then sped down the street.

"Are you okay?" Ned asked Nancy, resting his arm firmly against her back.

She nodded, unaware of deep bruises on her knees. "But I lost one of the smugglers!"

"No, you didn't."

"What?"

"You didn't." Seeing the bewilderment on Nancy's face, he squeezed her affectionately. "Look over there." He pointed to a crowd that had formed on the opposite block.

Nancy noticed George's head bob into view and spurred Ned to walk faster. When they reached the scene, she learned that two men who had seen Isakos push her into the street had tackled him and called the police. Isakos was sputtering in Greek.

"He threw me into the street on purpose!" Nancy told the policeman, but he did not understand her. Frustrated, she looked around quickly, calling out. "Can anyone translate for me?"

A university student stepped forward and in Greek repeated to the policeman what Nancy had said.

"Tell him this man is a thief and one of the art smugglers the authorities have been looking for. All they have to do is contact the archeological museum to confirm it."

"Nonsense," Isakos bellowed in her ear. "Pure rubbish."

"Like that basket of apples one of your pals sent you?" Nancy said, narrowing her eyes.

He laughed loudly, interrupting the student before he could translate her statement into Greek.

"Maybe you don't know about the snake in the basket," Nancy admitted. "After all, it wasn't delivered to your room, even though I'm positive it was meant for you!" She turned to the student again. "Tell the policeman I'm pressing charges against this man for trying to injure me! And this is not the first time, either. He tampered with my car, which could have resulted in a serious accident!"

Isakos glared at her. "You'll pay for this!" he blustered.

"On the contrary," Ned cut in, "you will."

When the six young people finally returned to the hotel, Mr. Drew and Helen were sharing their news with Mrs. Thompson.

"Vatis confessed," Helen said.

"He falsified records and forged Constantine's signature," Mr. Drew added.

"Even my uncle's, in order to get hold of the inheritance money," Helen concluded.

"Did he spend all of it?" Nancy asked.

"Fortunately, no. A valuable coin collection worth a great deal was kept in my uncle's safe-deposit box. Vatis never found the key to it, but kept paying for the rental. It was only a month ago that he told Constantine to take over the bills."

"I guess he figured he had enough money to live on for a while," Bess said. "What a greedy man!"

The next day, it was decided that she and Dave would take Helen and Mr. Drew to St. Mark's monastery.

"Constantine is waiting there for you both,"

Nancy told them. "Please don't be too rough on him, Dad."

"If I didn't know better," George said, "I'd suspect you were interested in the guy."

"Hardly," Nancy said. "Maybe I'm just a marshmallow at heart." She grinned.

"In that case," Ned remarked, "let's go out and have sundaes!"

"After we go to Piraeus," the girl detective replied.

She telephoned the harbor police requesting them to meet her group at the white-banded freighter.

"I thought the mystery was solved," Ned sighed as he drove up to the dock.

"Which one?" George laughed.

"There's always more than one, don't you know!" Burt added.

Ned turned off the ignition and the foursome got out.

"The freighter's leaving!" Nancy exclaimed.

"And there's Isakos's friend," George said.

"The same one who dragged Stella away from us," Nancy added as an Interpol agent arrived with the police. "We must stop that ship," Nancy said.

The men ran along the dock to a patrol boat and jumped in quickly. Nancy and Ned followed.

"We'll wait here for you!" George called.

The small craft churned through the water, catching up to the freighter in record time. The police ordered it to stop immediately.

"Hang on to me," Ned told Nancy as their boat pulled close to the ship. It rocked against the hull and the Interpol agent caught hold of a rope ladder. He climbed up first, followed by Nancy and Ned, then the police.

"What is the meaning of this?" Fotis questioned.

"You are under arrest," the Interpol agent said.

"On what grounds?"

"Shipping stolen goods."

"That man's involved, too," Nancy declared, pointing to Isakos's associate. "You're Dimitri Georgiou. Correct?"

"So what?" he snapped.

"You helped hide stolen artifacts from the museum in bales of cotton stored below deck," Nancy accused.

Although she and the police had checked a few random crates earlier and found nothing, her father had learned from museum authorities in the States that artifacts shipped from Greece were discovered in bales of cotton.

"I have nothing to say about that," Dimitri said.

"How does it feel to have taken money that was meant to help poor families?" Nancy asked him.

"I don't know what you're talking about!" Dimi-

157

tri hissed, but the crimson color in his face assured Nancy that she was right.

"You're also the one who abducted George on Corfu, aren't you?" she went on.

Dimitri stared at her full of anger.

"How did he get to Corfu?" Ned asked. "Just a little while ago, he ran a fake charity in the United States. Then all of a sudden he was in Corfu with Vatis?"

"That's because his real name is Dimitri Vatis!" Nancy said. "He's Vatis's brother and former partner. The original law firm consisted of Vatis Senior and two sons, not just one."

"How did you ever figure that out?"

"His money clip provided the clue. Remember, it had the initials *D.V.* on it—*V* for Vatis."

"Did you wiretap my phone, too?" the man rasped furiously.

"No need to," Nancy replied. "Your reaction just now was enough proof. Either you had an argument with your brother and left the law firm for that reason or you believed that running the Photini Agency in New York would be more lucrative. Then, when you realized that the police might soon uncover your scheme, you returned to Athens."

"That's when you found out about your brother's connection with Constantine and the Nicholas inheritance," Ned added.

"See if any of this holds up in court," the man sneered.

"Oh, it will," Nancy siad, "because Constantine will testify to everything."

"I'm also positive that Isakos will have a few things to say," George remarked.

"Especially since you and he stole the mosaics from St. Mark's monastery," Nancy said.

"Too bad we got in your way," Ned remarked.

"That wasn't the first time," George pointed out. "The night the three of us went to investigate St. Mark's, you or Isakos set off that weird noise in the gardens to distract us."

"It went on by mistake," Dimitri declared.

"Sending that poisonous snake to Isakos didn't work, either," Nancy went on. Her listener grumbled, but did not deny her accusation.

"Why did he do that?" Ned inquired.

"He wanted to get rid of Isakos and take over his racket," Nancy explained, "which, by the way, took Isakos to the U.S. on occasion. We happened to meet him on one of his return flights on Olympic Airways."

"When did Dimitri become involved with Isakos?"

"He learned about him from his brother, who in turn was aware of the art smuggling scheme through Constantine. When Dimitri returned to

Athens, he needed a job. He contacted Isakos. It didn't take him long to decide to take over Isakos's organization."

"Do you think Isakos realized what Dimitri was up to?" Ned asked.

"No. They worked closely together. As a matter of fact, the snake symbol was Dimitri's idea. He threw the smugglers' stamp at me in the hotel corridor."

"But why would he throw evidence in your path?"

"To plant something conclusive on me. He figured he could have me arrested and out of the way, once and for all." She paused, digging into her purse. "I don't plan to keep anything that will indict the man. Here." She handed Dimitri's money clip and the stamp to the agent from Interpol.

The police ordered Fotis to return his ship to the dock, where it would be searched. When they arrived, Dimitri and Fotis were led off in handcuffs.

"Thanks to you girls," the Interpol agent said, "the main members of the gang are now in tow!"

That evening, when Nancy's group was all together again, the young detectives and their dates took turns telling about Isakos's and Dimitri's capture.

"And to think I missed it all," Mrs. Thompson

said. "But I have to admit I did buy some lovely presents for the Papadapoulos family."

"That's great," Nancy replied.

"What about Constantine?" Nancy asked Helen.

"Your father has arranged something wonderful for him."

Mr. Drew smiled. "Well, it turned out that his role in the gang was a minor one. He didn't actually steal anything. He was just a go-between and delivery boy. For that, the gang gave him a reward once—the cuff bracelet. Unfortunately, he had been living way beyond his means and lost his job. That's when Isakos enlisted him with the promise of a lot of money."

"Which he never got, of course," Helen added.

"Right. That's why he gave Vatis the bracelet as payment for legal fees. Vatis realized it was a valuable ancient piece and pressed Constantine to tell him how he got it."

"What about Stella?" Bess asked. "She acted so peculiar when I met her in the dress shop. Obviously she knew Dimitri—"

"As a result of being Constantine's girlfriend," Mr. Drew said. "Dimitri began making deliveries to Chrysoteque, the jewelry shop, when Constantine stopped. Apparently, Dimitri told Stella he would harm Constantine if she even spoke to you girls, much less ask for your help."

"No wonder she pretended not to know me while I was shopping," Bess said.

"Well," Mr. Drew spoke up, "I convinced Constantine to turn himself in. He'll be out shortly on light bail."

"You're terrific, Dad," Nancy said, hugging him.

"I say this calls for a celebration," Helen declared. "I'm going to plan one on my new yacht."

"Your new yacht?" Nancy asked, surprised.

Helen explained that shortly before his death her uncle had ordered one to be built. It was ready now.

"What a shame he never had a chance to sail on it," Bess remarked.

"But we will tomorrow!" Helen said gaily.

The following day, she led the group to a berth near the Nikos dock. The yacht, nearly two hundred feet long from bow to stern, glistened in the sunlight.

"She's gorgeous!" Nancy exclaimed.

Suddenly, she noticed the crest on the bow. It was identical to the one on the silver box the young priest had left at the church in Plaka!

"That's the Nikos crest!" Nancy exclaimed.

Bess and George stared in amazement. "You mean the priest we saw on our first afternoon in Greece was Constantine?" Bess asked.

"That's correct," Mr. Drew replied. "He told me

162

he gave the silver box that had been in his possession for a long time to his patron saint—to make up for his dishonest ways."

"Now, no more talk of such unpleasant things," Helen interrupted. "Someone must christen this boat for me. Will you, Carson?"

"I'd be happy to," the lawyer said. "What are you going to call it?"

"Well, since I wouldn't have had it without your daughter's help, I'm calling it the *Nancy Drew!*"

The girl sleuth was stunned into grateful silence. Now that her exciting adventure had come to an end, she found herself daydreaming about her next one. She did not yet know it would begin soon when she discovered *The Swami's Ring*.

Seeing the glow on Nancy's face, Helen continued. "Giving someone's name to a ship is the highest honor a shipping family in Greece can bestow on anyone. But then, you are the most wonderful young detective in the world!"

JOIN NANCY DREW
AT THE COUNTRY CLUB!

You can be a charter member of Nancy Drew's River Heights Country Club™— Join today! Be a part of the wonderful, exciting and adventurous world of River Heights, USA™.

You'll get four issues of the Country Club's quarterly newsletter with valuable advice from the nation's top experts on make-up, fashion, dating, romance, and how to take charge and plan your future. Plus, you'll get a complete River Heights, USA, Country Club™ membership kit containing an official ID card for your wallet, an 8-inch full color iron-on transfer, a laminated bookmark, 25 sticker seals, and a beautiful enamel pin of the Country Club logo.

It's a retail value of over $12. But, as a charter member, right now you can get in on the action for only $5.00. So, fill out and mail the coupon and a check or money order now. *Please do not send cash.* Then get ready for the most exciting adventure of your life!

MAIL TO: Nancy Drew's River Heights Country Club
House of Hibbert   CN-4609
Trenton, NJ 08650

Here's my check or money order for $5.00! I want to be a charter member of the exciting new Nancy Drew's River Heights, USA Country Club™.

Name _____ Age _____

Address _____

City _____ State _____ ZIP _____

Allow six to eight weeks for delivery.   NDDC6

144